A Story Every Day of WINTER

Edited by John Howes and Fran Neatherway

Copyright © 2023 The Rugby Cafe Writers.
Copyright remains with the individual writers of each story. All rights reserved.

This book or any portion thereof may not be reproduced or used in any manner whatsoever without the express written permission of the publisher except for the use of brief quotations in a book review.
Printed in the United Kingdom.

This is a work of fiction. Unless otherwise indicated, all the names, characters, businesses, places, events and incidents in this book are either the product of the author's imagination or used in a fictitious manner. Any resemblance to actual persons, living or dead, or actual events is purely coincidental.

First Printing, 2023

ISBN: 9798865664222
Imprint: Independently published

For more information about The Cafe Writers of Rugby, visit their website, www.rugbycafewriters.com

The text of this book is set in Georgia, 10.5pt. This is a typeface designed in 1993 specifically for reading on computer screens and named after a bizarre newspaper headline, *Alien heads found in Georgia*. It has since become increasingly popular and was adopted by *The New York Times* in 2007.

Introduction

The Glory Of Winter

I'm sure we are all familiar with Christina Rossetti's poem which talks of the "bleak mid-winter" when "frosty wind made moan". There is a sense of stark coldness and struggle about it all, and when the days of autumn are receding and the icy mornings are with us, it is easy to identify with Rossetti's images of a difficult winter ahead.

However, some people find this to be their favourite time of the year. There can be a cosiness to the winter providing you are fortunate enough to have a warm home which you enjoy; even more so if you find within that place a quiet corner, and a comfortable armchair where you can relax in comfort and enjoy reading a favourite book. Nothing can replace the touch and feel of a real book, whether you prefer softback or hardback, and all the potential contained within its as-yet unread pages. What secrets will it reveal to you? Who will be your favourite character? How will the author entertain you and how will they give you that satisfied feeling at the end of a story when you don't want to be parted from the characters and can't wait to find out if there will be a sequel?

We hope you will have some of the same feelings when you read this collection of short stories. This is the third of our seasonal anthologies. So far, we have published anthologies for summer and autumn. Here is winter, and the cycle will be completed by the spring collection due out around February time.

The Cafe Writers of Rugby were formed as a group about six years ago. Most of us live in the Midlands town of Rugby in the United Kingdom. We come from all walks of life, with different backgrounds and interests - but we have one thing in common: we love writing. So we get together in a cafe once a fortnight and share our latest work. We often have a Writing Challenge and you will find several stories in this collection with the same beginning, "Do you believe in Father

Christmas?" We hope you will enjoy the different ways in which writers have answered this question.

This book gives you a story for every day of December, January and February, with themes including Christmas, New Year, winter in general, Valentine's Day and Leap Year.

If you enjoy the collection, please consider buying another in the series and, if you enjoy writing, please visit our website and get in touch with us. We would love to hear from you.

John Howes
www.rugbycafewriters.com

Contents

Introduction **The Glory Of Winter** John Howes — 4

December

December 1 **Reindeer Talking** David J Boulton — 11
December 2 **Brief Encounter** John Howes — 12
December 3 **Christmas To Do** Christine Hancock — 13
December 4 **Pre-Christmas Lunch** Madalyn Morgan — 14
December 5 **A Tale Of Two Cities** Simon Parker — 15
December 6 **The Paper Cut-Out** Wendy Goulstone — 16
December 7 **Christmas Game** Chris Wright — 17
December 8 **Peter and Jane** Jim Hicks — 18
December 9 **Passing It On** Wendy Goulstone — 19
December 10 **The Big Question** EE Blythe — 21
December 11 **Do You Believe?** Fran Neatherway — 22
December 12 **The Book Signing** John Howes — 23
December 13 **Carol Singing** Jim Hicks — 24
December 14 **Believing** Steve Redshaw — 25
December 15 **The Holly Bears A Thorn** Wendy Goulstone — 26
December 16 **The Night Before Christmas** Kate A. Harris — 31
December 17 **Charlotte Hannah** EE Blythe — 33
December 18 **The Week Before Christmas** Wendy Goulstone — 34
December 19 **Christmas On Mars** Simon Grenville — 35
December 20 **Disaster Averted** Lindsay Woodward — 36
December 21 **They Say It Was Christmas** Wendy Goulstone — 37
December 22 **Sleigh Bells** Fran Neatherway — 38
December 23 **Christmas Traditions** Madalyn Morgan — 40
December 24 **The Night Before Christmas** Fran Neatherway — 43
December 25 **Father Christmas** Lindsay Woodward — 45
December 26 **Mince Pies** Theresa Le Flem — 47
December 27 **Snow** Fran Neatherway — 48
December 28 **Wonderful Christmas Time** Chris Wright — 49
December 29 **The Festive Spirit** Christopher Trezise — 51

December 30 **The Snowflake Makers** Chloe Huntington 54
December 31 **Blue, With Stars** EE Blythe 58

January

January 1 **This Year** Jim Hicks 63
January 2 **A New Beginning** Steve Redshaw 64
January 3 **A Christmas Character** Chris Rowe 66
January 4 **What Do You Mean I Can't Come?** Rosemary Marks 67
January 5 **Relative Values** Fran Neatherway 73
January 6 **A Village Christmas** Ruth Hughes 79
January 7 **A Feltwell Christmas** David G Bailey 81
January 8 **Jane's Terror** Lindsay Woodward 85
January 9 **The Abbey Hotel** Wendy Goulstone 87
January 10 **Gold** John Howes 95
January 11 **'Panic' Isn't In The Geordie Dialect** Chris Rowe 97
January 12 **Ninety-One** Ruth Hughes 101
January 13 **Matilda And The Little Blue Dog** Chris Wright 102
January 14 **The Fate Of Fifty-Two** Lindsay Woodward 104
January 15 **In The Mist** Wendy Goulstone 106
January 16 **The Last Second** EE Blythe 111
January 17 **Calm Attic Spaghetti** Cathy Hemsley 113
January 18 **Alter Ego** Chris Rowe 118
January 19 **Winter** Patrick Garrett 120
January 20 **La Belle Epoque** John Howes 123
January 21 **Trying To Make It** Wendy Goulstone 125
January 22 **Cliff Hanger** Lindsay Woodward 127
January 23 **Teapot** Fran Neatherway 129
January 24 **He Said 'Hi'** EE Blythe 133
January 25 **The Fifth Valley** Chris Rowe 135
January 26 **Hope** Ruth Hughes 137
January 27 **The Cuckoo In The Nest** Fran Neatherway 138
January 28 **Old Man And Dog** John Howes 141
January 29 **Illness** Lindsay Woodward 143
January 30 **Red Wellies** EE Blythe 145
January 31 **Black Water, Blue Wine** Chris Wright 147

February

February 1 **Inspiration** Kate A. Harris	151
February 2 **Penthouse Omega** Chris Wright	155
February 3 **Hope** Rosemary Marks	157
February 4 **And It Shall Come To Pass** Wendy Goulstone	159
February 5 **Eight** Christopher Trezise	163
February 6 **The Saga Of The Ashes** Ruth Hughes	166
February 7 **The Problem With Writing** Chris Rowe	167
February 8 **Beliefs Of Vikings** Chloe Huntington	169
February 9 **Red Letters** Chris Wright	173
February 10 **Number One** Rosemary Marks	175
February 11 **Miss Darling** John Howes	177
February 12 **Salad Sandwiches** Ruth Hughes	179
February 13 **My Valentine** Lindsay Woodward	180
February 14 **Ships That Pass** EE Blythe	182
February 15 **The Kiss** Wendy Goulstone	183
February 16 **Wedding Vows** Rosemary Marks	191
February 17 **Big Spender** Fran Neatherway	197
February 18 **A Good Story, But I Don't Believe A Word Of It** Philip Gregge	203
February 19 **Togetherness** Chris Wright	205
February 20 **Temptation** John Howes	208
February 21 **Carrots** Lindsay Woodward	210
February 22 **My Lucky Number** Patrick Garrett	212
February 23 **Lovebite** Ruth Hughes	213
February 24 **Homecoming** Jim Hicks	214
February 25 **Return To The Crematorium** EE Blythe	215
February 26 **My Short True Story** Patrick Garrett	217
February 27 **1968** EE Blythe	219
February 28 **Love In A Leap Year** Ruth Hughes	220
February 29 **Birthdays** Fran Neatherway	221
About the authors	226

A Story for Every Day of Winter

December

A Story for Every Day of Winter

December 1

Reindeer Talking

'Twas the week before Christmas...

"Bloody Hell, it's not that time again is it?"

To the doubters amongst you, it may come as a surprise that reindeer can talk, but then, they're careful not to be heard in human company; not even if it's dressed up in a ridiculous red suit.

"I don't suppose the old fool has had a shave since last year."

The little herd stood together in a huddle. Anyone looking on might have seen Dasher, Prancer and the rest. I mean, would you talk to people who'd given you such stupid labels?

"Why do we put up with it each year?" said Blitzen, complaining again. "I mean, we should be out there snuffling about in the snow for lichens with the others."

As a narrator, and not one of them, I was instructed not to name them, but what the hell; it was Cupid who said, "That's just it. Do you really want to be sticking your nose into the snow? Mine gets chapped."

"It's for the food they give us; is that what you're saying?" It was Comet this time.

"And from what I've heard, there isn't going to be much more of that. Haven't you heard of Amazon?"

David J Boulton

December 2

Brief Encounter

It was a few weeks before Christmas. She had something in her eye - and he was a doctor, after all. So it seemed perfectly natural that he would lay hands on her. The grit was soon removed. A drunken Father Christmas gazed on this brief encounter on the station platform, a poignant moment, bound to change lives. The brass brand struck up *Silent Night* as the couple headed for the buffet. Teacups in hand, they found a corner table.

Following a comfortable silence, she said, "I'm married."

"So am I," he replied.

Should they? Shouldn't they? Worlds turn upside down on more trivial exchanges.

His train was called. Their fingers touched, their eyes met, their lips trembled. This couldn't be. Think of the children.

The train approached.

"We can't," she insisted.

"You're right," he said. "Too much to lose."

The band played on. Still, their fingers rested on the table, tip to tip. Everything else was in the past. Was it selfishness, or the truest love in the world?

He withdrew his hand.

And touched her face.

John Howes

Inspired by the 1945 classic film, Brief Encounter, written by Noel Coward and directed by David Lean.

December 3

Christmas To Do

'Twas the week before Christmas and I'd lost my list.

No, not that one, that's the card list, out of date now, except for that round robin from someone called Bill.

Bill who? His or mine? Leave it for now, too late to reply, whoever he is.

Two lists for the supermarket, this week and next, which is which? When to go? Is Christmas Eve too late?

Those lists are menus, one for each day, I don't know why I write them, they're the same every year.

The present lists. No! Don't even go there.

I need the list for the market. There, hidden beneath yet another recipe for stuffing.

Chipolatas and sausage meat, streaky bacon and a gammon joint. Every bit of a pig. How about a boar's head? No, don't be silly.

Turkey! Will they have a turkey? If I get it now, will the weather be icy, or must I find room in the bulging fridge? Should I get it from Sainsbury's, will there be any left?

Eggs! Eggs? No, it's Christmas, not Easter.

Don't panic! Calm down. There's plenty of time. A whole week to go.

Mustn't forget to take out the giblets.

Don't worry, I'll start another list.

Christine Hancock

December 4

Pre-Christmas Lunch

It was the week before Christmas when Alison's new boss telephoned.

'Who was that?' Peter asked when she returned to the sitting room.

'Dee Saunders, from the office. She and Simon have invited us round for a pre-Christmas lunch. I said we'd go.'

'When?'

'Tomorrow.'

'Oh, no!'

'Why not? Dee's lovely and you'll like her husband Simon.'

'Will I?'

'Like you he was at Oxford, and he's also a lawyer.'

Yes, Peter thought, who didn't think I was good enough to work for his law firm. 'I can't tomorrow, darling, I'm going to a partners' meeting.'

'Since when?'

'Since Sir John emailed. Lunch at his club to discuss my promotion. I have to go.'

'Of course. A promotion? I'll telephone Dee and tell her,' Alison said leaving the room.

Relieved that he no longer had to see the arrogant Simon Saunders, Peter opened a bottle of his best wine and poured two glasses.

'It's fine,' Alison said on her return, 'Dee and Simon are coming here for a pre-Christmas lunch on Sunday. Ooh, my favourite wine. You spoil me. What shall we drink to?' Alison raised her glass. 'I know, to new friends!'

Madalyn Morgan

December 5

A Tale Of Two Cities

'Twas the week before Christmas and Jim Adams was on the Eurostar back from Paris, after a week-long business trip.

It was just after Christmas ten years ago that his father had died, and he'd been thinking about him a lot this past week. He always made an enormous fuss about Christmas and loved every minute of it.

An older gentleman was sitting opposite, and he smiled as Jim sat down, saying, "Busy week?" Jim rolled his eyes and smiled back, saying, "Just mad, but it's over now."

Jim had an overwhelming feeling of calm and wellbeing talking with the man but after a while, closed his eyes. He woke up with a start in an otherwise empty carriage, with the train stopped in St. Pancras Station.

Jim noticed a shabby copy of *A Tale Of Two Cities*, one of his favourite books, on the seat opposite.

I have to catch the man and return his book, thought Jim. Fully awake now, he leapt off the train and ran down the platform, but there was no sign. Sorry that he'd missed him, Jim opened the book.

On the inside of the cover was a hand-written inscription: *Happy Christmas 2010, Jim. All my love, Dad xx*

Simon Parker

December 6

The Paper Cut-Out

Do you believe in Father Christmas?

Of course I believe. He and I get on well, sharing the work. I see to the people on my list; he serves all the other believers in the rest of the world, and he always leaves me a little something as a thank you gift.

One year, during the war, I doubted his existence. I asked for a doll, but he left a little paper cut-out lying in a cardboard box, about twice the size of a Swan Vesta matchbox, with a piece of pink felt for a cover. I still have this tiny blanket somewhere, as a reminder. The paper doll disintegrated.

That year he must have been short of money, struggling to make ends meet and living on meagre rations, like the rest of us. Those wartime years were difficult for my family, too, but I still remember the disappointment that Christmas morning as I sat eating a slice of toast, spread thickly with dripping, for my breakfast.

Now I begin to wonder if he will give in his resignation, as children are requesting too many expensive items in their Christmas letters. Perhaps he should deliver paper dolls again.

Wendy Goulstone

December 7

Christmas Game

"Do you believe in Father Christmas, Sarah?" teased Kate.

Early December and the three sisters sat round the old kitchen table and listened intently for the Yuletide songs, switching between channels to speed things up. No kids or partners were allowed in the room, just La Vieille Ferme Rosé and three glasses.

"It's called *I believe in Father Christmas*," replied Sarah sternly, "and the game is on. Your turn, Sue."

DAB blasted *Fairy-Tale Of New York*. Wine top ups all round.

"Your turn, Kate, and you're a cheap lousy maggot for suggesting this game."

Now it played *Stop The Cavalry*. "Bub-a dub a dub. And I'm clear," crowed Kate. "Your turn, Sarah."

All I Want For Christmas Is You.

"Your turn, Sue."

I Wish it Could Be Christmas Every Day, *Merry Christmas Everybody*, *Do They Know It's Christmas*? They chopped and changed between the Christmas pop-up stations.

Eventually, Magic Christmas played *Jingle Bell Rock*.

"Your turn, Sarah."

The radio played *Rocking Around The Christmas Tree*.

"Your turn, Sue."

The DAB blasted *Merry Christmas Everyone*.

"Your turn, Kate."

At last they heard *Last Christmas*.

"Damn!" cried Kate.

"Whamageddon!!" chorused Sue and Sarah

"Ok. Mum can stay at my house Christmas and Boxing Day," laughed Kate.

Chris Wright

December 8

Peter and Jane

"Do you believe in Father Christmas?"

"No!" cried Natasha, stamping her foot.

Peter and Jane exchanged a knowing look.

"Tash, we need to go to your bedroom and have a talk," said Jane, leading Natasha out of the playroom.

Natasha's tantrums never lasted long.

In the bedroom, Jane explained, "Tash, many children and grown-ups like to pretend that Father Christmas exists and comes to bring presents on Christmas Eve. They think it's fun. Jonathan still believes in Father Christmas, so at least pretend that you do."

Natasha looked pensive for a few seconds. "Do I still get a Christmas stocking?"

"Yes."

"All right."

Jane brought Natasha back to the playroom, where Peter was playing with Vanessa and Jonathan.

Peter and Jane exchanged another look. They had had the same talk with Vanessa five years before, and they knew they would do the same with Jonathan in about three years.

Jim Hicks

December 9

Passing It On

Bob woke early, yawned, looked at the alarm clock. No time for an extra doze today. He fought his way out of the blankets and sat on the side of the bed, feeling for his slippers.

Thank goodness for central heating. No more feathery ice patterns on the windows like when he was a kid in a Victorian two-up two-down terraced house in the back streets. He grabbed his stick and pottered to the bathroom. No need to trim his beard today.

The taxi arrived in good time. He rummaged in his pockets to pay the fare and flip-flopped along the path to the door that led to the children's ward.

'Happy Christmas Santa,' said the receptionist, and handed him the costume and the sack.

'The presents are all uni-sex, suit any age group, just to make it easy for you. The children are more lively this morning, poor little things. Have fun! That cubicle there is free for you to change in. I'll watch your clothes for you. You know the way, don't you? Oh, and here is the bell. Can you manage it with your walking stick as well?'

'I'll leave my stick with my clothes,' said Santa. 'I'll be fine.'

Ten minutes later, Santa adjusted the hood, tightened the belt, put the bag over his shoulder and plodded along the corridor, jingling the bell in time with his steps.

'Oh, children, listen,' announced the nurse on guard by the door.

'Can you hear anything?'

Santa rang the bell vigorously.

'Sh! Sh! Be quiet and I'll open the door and see who it is.'

A general shouting and screaming greeted Santa as he stepped into the room.

'Merry Christmas, children,' sang out Santa. 'Merry Christmas, boys and girls.'

'Merry Christmas!' shouted the children, the ones who had not hidden under the bedclothes.

'Now, let me see what is in my sack,' said Santa. 'I do hope my elves have packed enough presents for everybody.'

The children fell silent, each hoping they would be one of the lucky ones. Santa went round the beds, asking names and handing out the presents, and, of course, there were enough, and soon there was just a rustling of wrapping paper and squeals of delight.

'I mustn't forget the staff,' said Santa. He fished out a box of chocolates for each, and received a traditional kiss from each giggling nurse.

'Goodbye, everyone, goodbye, until next year!'

In the corridor Santa leant against the wall, his head spinning. He was getting too old for this game. The sooner he was at home, the happier he would be. His son-in-law was going to pick him up from the hospital to spend the rest of the day at their place. Great. Not much chance of a snooze after dinner, though. They'd be playing all sorts of mad games, the grandchildren making a racket and the dog barking. Better get going and change back into his own clothes, so he was ready.

+ +

'How are you, Dad? No, don't sit up. Just lie still. Well, fancy you ending up in here on Christmas Day. How do you feel? Still a bit dizzy? That was a nasty fall you had. I should let a younger chap do the job next year, then you can spend the whole day with us, no worries.'

The sound of jingle bells was heard in the corridor.

'Looks like you have visitors, Dad.'

And in came Santa, followed by the ladies from the local Women's Institute choir.

'Happy Christmas!' said Santa.

'Happy Christmas, Santa!' said Bob.

Wendy Goulstone

December 10
The Big Question

"Do you believe in Father Christmas?"

"Eh, what?"

"Father Christmas, do you believe in him?"

"In what way?"

"What do you mean 'in what way'?"

Exasperated sigh, and short silence.

"Do you believe in Father Christmas?"

"Depends."

"On what?"

"Do I believe Father Christmas exists, has always existed? Or, do I believe in Father Christmas as some sort of faith system super-being? That sort of 'depends'. What do you mean?"

Exasperated sigh. Short silence.

"I'm not going to talk to you!" And he turned on his heel and marched off to the kitchen.

"Hello," said a deep voice from among the rattle of pans and roasting tins.

And in a resigned tone, came the words,

"Do you believe in Father Christmas?"

EE Blythe

December 11

Do You Believe?

"Do you believe in Father Christmas?"

"Yes. On Christmas night Father Christmas brings presents to everyone." She twisted in her seat. The light was very bright and made her eyes hurt.

"How does he do that?"

"He has a sledge pulled by reindeers. They fly through the sky. Father Christmas goes down the chimney with the presents. The reindeers' names are Dancer and Prancer, Cupid and Comet, Donner and Blitzen." She giggled. "Mummy says that means Thunder and Lightning, but Daddy says it's Damn and Blast."

"If there isn't a chimney?"

"Magic? Mummy puts out mince pies and a glass of milk, and carrots for the reindeers. In the morning they're gone." She rubbed her tummy.

"In every house?"

"That's why he's so fat!"

"One human delivers presents to everyone in the world on one night – by himself?"

"Yes, but only if you're good. If you're naughty, he brings you a lump of coal instead. Can I go now?"

The interrogator pressed a button and the child disappeared.

His head swivelled and he said to the watchers, "I have questioned many humans and they all say the same thing. If one human can do all this in one night, then I fear we will not be successful in conquering Earth."

The alien fleet abandoned their invasion and set off on their long voyage home. The interrogator hoped Father Christmas would bring him a piece of coal. He was hungry.

Fran Neatherway

December 12

The Book Signing

Do you believe in Father Christmas? was the title of my new book.

A pile of them sat on the table in front of me untouched.

It was Christmas Eve and I was doing a meet-the-author session at Waterstone's in Oxford Street, London, my favourite bookshop in the whole world.

Except no-one wanted to read the book or meet me.

My apparent proof that Father Christmas didn't exist wasn't proving attractive. Neither was I. My partner had left me, my dog was on the way out. Christmas would be alone. No love, no magic.

The clock ticked on ominously.

I looked around, sighed, tapped my feet. A minute until closing. Then, 'Did you write this?' said a woman's voice.

I looked up. A vision of intelligence, beauty and warmth.

'I'd been hoping to meet you. It sounds fascinating,' she said.

This was going well.

'Have you got time for a chat?' she asked.

Had I? You bet.

Somewhere in the distance, sleigh bells rang and a deep voice boomed, 'Me-rrry Christmas'.

John Howes

December 13

Carol Singing

I had never seen the point of going carol singing.

Partly this was because of the scene in the film *Love Actually* where a man calls on the woman he wants to flatter, turns on a recording of carols and holds up a notice reading TELL HIM IT'S CAROL SINGERS.

I always thought this contrived. Well, that and I was thinking, who is Carol Singers?

Still, I had somehow been bamboozled into going round the village singing carols on Christmas Eve. It took about an hour and it wasn't too cold.

We finished at the home of Old Mother Bates and her daughters. John, our leader, told us to sing *We Wish You a Merry Christmas*.

We all like our figgy pudding.

We all like our figgy pudding.

We all like our figgy pudding, so bring some out here.

And we won't go until we've got some —

At this point Mother Bates and one of her daughters went inside.

And we won't go until we've got some.

And we won't go until we've got some, so bring some out here.

The two women re-appeared, carrying steaming trays. Hot figgy pudding.

It had, of course, all been arranged in advance.

Jim Hicks

December 14

Believing

Do you believe in Father Christmas?

Annie was the originator of our most solemn family mantra. She was eight, and when she asked the question, it was abundantly clear she expected nothing but the truth. And our answer was totally honest. At some time, somehow, that question came to represent the most serious and heartfelt request for the truth. And still, over thirty years later, it is our way of saying, 'Listen, no matter how hard or hurtful it may be, don't sidestep or avoid anything, just tell me the truth.'

This rather bizarre family code was last used one year ago, when the most precious, loving wife and mother anyone could wish for was diagnosed with terminal cancer. She was taken from us within a few weeks. It broke our hearts. From that awful moment Annie and I had been desperately and tearfully clinging to one another.

Yesterday, I had a lengthy hospital consultation. This afternoon Annie will visit. I can hear the concern and seriousness that will be in her voice as I try to rehearse the response I know I must deliver. I picture the pleading, but determined look her face will display, when she asks, 'Dad, do you believe in Father Christmas?'

Steve Redshaw

December 15

The Holly Bears A Thorn

The loft was stacked with boxes and trunks of stuff not wanted but too good to throw away. They should have got rid of it years ago but the bother of getting the tall stepladder out of the shed and standing it under the trap door, sliding the bolts and then scrambling up into the loft without the swinging trapdoor knocking them off the stepladder was too much of an effort. Terry had planked the joists, but they still hadn't arranged for a more convenient expanding ladder to be fitted. But here they were trying to find the Christmas decorations after several years of managing with a bit of holly and a few baubles on the mantelpiece.

'Look what I've found!' said Louise. 'That hideous ornament from Auntie Lucy! Our wedding present. One she'd had on her mantelpiece since 300 BC. I remember seeing it when I was a kid. I used to like it, the colours, I suppose. Do you think it is valuable?'

'No. Give it to Oxfam.'

'Oxfam won't want it, Terry. Who would buy a monstrosity like this?'

'Bin it, then.'

'I haven't the heart. Part of my childhood, this is. It can stay up here.'

Louise carefully replaced the monstrosity in its box and opened another.

'Why have you hoarded all this stuff, Louise? Look at all this kids' stuff. Why are you keeping it?'

'I was hoping Geraldine might want it, but there's still no sign of any babies.'

'And there will not be any, Louise. They are too busy with careers and making a packet, and jetting off all over the globe to want the encumbrance of a family.

'They need a break.'

'I never did like babies. She put a stop to our enjoyment of life. Everything had to be geared to Geraldine. What Geraldine wanted, Geraldine got. If I had my time again, I wouldn't have kids.'

'Terry! How can you say that? Our lovely daughter. Wishing her away like that.

'A kid wasn't my choice.'

'Look at all the joy we had, watching her growing up. Geraldine loved the seaside, camping in the Lakes, her birthday-parties.'

'You and Geraldine may have had fun. I didn't. Then the cost of seeing her through university. Free handouts from the Bank of Mum and Dad, ie Dad.'

'But, Terry, look at her now, how high she's flown. The money was worth it.'

'Not to me, it wasn't. When did she and her bloke last show their faces round here?

'They're busy.'

'Too busy to visit her parents?'

They're coming for Christmas lunch.'

'But then they're off back to their posh friends in Park Lane.'

'They don't live in Park Lane.'

'Buck House then.'

'Now you're being ridiculous, Terry.'

'The trouble with you, Louise, is that you can't see beyond the end of your nose. You don't see ulterior motives. You just believe everything anyone says.'

'I see what's good in people. I don't look for faults, like you do, Terry.

'You find plenty of faults in me, Louise'.

'That's different. I can read you like a book. I know what you're thinking.'

'Little do you know, Louise. Little do you know.'

And little she did know. She and Terry's conversations of late had degenerated into bickering. Either that or long silences. They turned back to searching the boxes.

'Terry, get that plastic box, there, fourth one down on that pile. I think the Christmas decorations are in there.'

Terry struggled with the toppling pile and dragged out the plastic box. Louise prised off the lid.

'Oh no, they're not. Sorry.'

'I don't know why you want to bother with decorations. You only have the palaver of putting them back again.'

'We want the house to look nice and cheerful for when they come.'

'No, we don't. And they won't notice decorations. They'll only be here for an hour, drinking my booze, and off they'll go with a bottle of whisky and half a Christmas cake on the back seat.'

'Geraldine's too busy to make her own. Anyway, I like her to have it. I make a big one specially.'

'You're wasting your time. They come, they go as soon as they can make their escape.'

'Do you know why they don't stay, Terry? They don't stay because Geraldine knows that you don't like her. You never have. Children can tell when someone dislikes them. You never played with her, not even at the seaside, never read bedtime stories.'

'I'm not listening to this. I'm going downstairs.'

'Before you go, see if the Christmas tree is behind that pile of boxes in the corner. Wrapped up in polythene sheeting, it should be. I think I can see it.'

The boxes weighed a ton. Some toppled down, showering dust on Terry's head.

'Be careful with them, Terry. I've put crockery we don't use in some of them.'

'If we don't use it, why do you keep it?'

'Well, you never know when we might need it. When there's a funeral and such.'

'And whose funeral are you planning, Louise?'

'I'm not planning anybody's funeral. But, if one of us…'

'Well, I'm not coming up here for extra plates.'

'Terry, That's not a nice thing to say! Have a look in that long parcel. I think the tree is in there.'

Terry tugged at the parcel. More boxes tottered. With much effort, muttering and swearing he unwrapped a large green sunshade.

'No, that's not it. Wrap it up again and put it back.'

'Do it yourself. I'm off downstairs. Forget the tree. Just put a sprig of holly on the table.'

'I like to brighten the house up. It's miserable enough for the rest of the year. You and me. There's no happiness in our lives.'

'What is there to be happy about? Come on, Louise. What is there to be happy about? Speak up. I can't hear you. What did you say, Louise?'

'You and me. What sort of life is this? This house is like a morgue. The only time there's a smile on my face is when I open the front door, walk into the street and breathe fresh air.'

'And the only time there's a smile on my face, Louise, is when you shut the door behind you.'

'I know how you feel about me, Terry. It wasn't always like this.'

'Oh, wasn't it? Are you sure about that, Louise? Do you think I would have married you if your father hadn't stood behind me with a shot gun?

'So you are blaming me, are you? I don't suppose you had anything to do with Geraldine's conception, did you?

'As a matter of fact, no, I didn't. I found out about your reputation at the reception, Louise. The blokes, after a few beers. Joking, I thought. But there was always that doubt in my mind right from the start. There's no-one in my family with red hair like the hair on Geraldine's head.'

'What are you suggesting?

'Now, let me see, Michael Scrivener, perhaps? Or his brother, Tony? Or their cousin, Graham Hurst?

'And you, you believed their lies, their jokes, did you, Terry? You've accused me of believing what people say. Now you are doing it. Just take a look at yourself, Terry. Are you the innocent, injured party? I know a thing or two about you, Terry. I know where you go on Tuesday evenings. And it isn't the Working Men's Club, is it, Terry? Why have you gone quiet, Terry? Cat got your tongue?'

'Spot on, Louise. And the cat is standing right in front of me. Yes, if you must know, I do have a close friend. She and I have known each other for years. Before I married you, Louise. Before you tricked me into sleeping with you, Louise. Before you tricked me into marriage, Louise. Graham Hurst being a married man already, Louise.'

'So what are you going to do, Terry? Go off to your bit on the side?'

'That is exactly what I'm going to do, Louise. As a matter of fact, we've already made plans to go somewhere no-one will find us.'

He went to the trapdoor, sat on the edge of the hole and lowered himself down to the stepladder.

'I'll leave you to find the Christmas tree, Louise. Geraldine will be able to take it home with her after she finds you. That's if she finds you. Happy Christmas, Louise.'

The trapdoor banged up against the frame. Terry slid the bolts into place.

The stepladder rattled as he folded it and carried it away.

'Terry!' Louise screamed.

She scrambled over boxes and banged on the trapdoor.

'Terry! Don't be an idiot. Terry, what are you doing? Let me out. Come on, Terry. Let me out.'

There was no answer.

'Terry! Terry" Open the door. Let me out, Terry. Terry, please. Open the door. Terry, please. Please.

She heard the front door bang and the roar of the car as he drove away down the road.

Wendy Goulstone

December 16

The Night Before Christmas

It was the night before Christmas. I slid the restraining arm of the ancient white painted shutter out of its holder, and let it swing back into the window of our Old Rectory.

Was that jingling Father Christmas and his reindeer flying overhead? That's what I wanted to know. Father had placed three mince pies and a glass of sherry on the dressing table for them. Surely it wouldn't be long before they visited.

I was seven years old, I think. It was a long, long time ago.

It was the coldest night of the year. I breathed heavily onto the window pane to melt Jack Frost's thick frosty patterns, inside the window. We didn't have heating in our bedrooms in the mid-1950s. Darkness and cold grabbed me. It was a freezing cold night with stars twinkling brightly in the cloudless sky.

Street lights weren't seen in the small country village and the stars seemed bigger back then filling the expanse of darkness.

I couldn't see Santa. Excited, I wondered whether all the reindeer would be pulling Santa's sleigh. My sister was sleeping, her soft regular snores. I didn't want to be alone when Father Christmas visited, although I didn't want her to wake.

There was a scraping on the window. Cupping my hands around wide staring eyes, I peered into the night sky and began to imagine what the noise could be outside the glass. I could see it was only a branch of a rose bush up the side of the house, a sharp end of which was slowly brushing across the window in a slight breeze.

Quickly I pulled the shutters across and, together, let the heavy restrainer fall onto its clip to fasten them shut, pulled my dressing gown tightly around my cold body and ran back to my bed. My feet were soon cosy warm in my new pink Christmas socks.

The bed was cold as I curled up, moving my legs up and down

trying to keep warm.

Diana was still fast asleep snoring away, oblivious of me walking around and I couldn't wait to go to sleep, as I knew Father Christmas wouldn't call if I wasn't.

I lay my head on the freezing pillow. The scraping of the oak branch had stopped and the room was silent.

Then light was showing through the gaps around the shutters and I knew it must be morning. Thankfully I'd slept through the night. I jumped up to put the light on.

At that moment my sister sat up and said:

'He's been. Father Christmas has been. Look, the stockings are bulging with presents. Quick, let's look.'

There was chocolate money in golden wrappers and a small bar of chocolate, a tangerine, rubber, ruler, pencil sharpener, a special two-sized metal sharpener, a box of six coloured pencils, a small notepad, a hanky with my initial C and the main present a doll, called Caroline; she was made of soft plastic with tight blond, wiry hair and a brightly made up face, quite scary thinking back to then. Also there was *Noddy Gets Into Trouble* by Enid Blyton and one of the first books that I loved to read.

Another exciting Christmas morning and time to show our presents to Mummy and Daddy! Happy Christmas.

Kate A. Harris

December 17

Charlotte Hannah

She didn't know what she wanted for Christmas, so hadn't been able to tell the large man in red anything. But a soft voice from a nearby counter caught her attention, and held her.

Talking dolls. Dolls that could talk to each other, or to people, without pulling a string or pressing a button. She stood transfixed, just talking to the doll, until her hand was taken and she was led away.

Christmas Day morning came early. Very early. Barely ninety minutes after both parents had sunk thankfully onto a soft mattress, beneath a thick duvet.

"Oh, he's been!" came one voice.

"And me," shouted another. And then came the sound of footsteps along the landing, accompanied by the unmistakable sounds of something being dragged. A groan escaped the father. But he was feigning sleep when the children came in, climbed onto the bed, and began to show them both what Father Christmas had brought.

The talking doll added to the noise as she went through all her phrases, responding to the volume of sound, and to movement. And when every book, car, flashing gizmo and bag of jelly beans had been looked at and admired, the children were persuaded to go back to bed until the sun came up.

Peace at last for the parents, but not for long. There was a burbling noise every so often. A murmuring, until . . .

"She won't shut up," wailed a small voice from the next bedroom.

"Now you know how we feel," her father replied, turning on his side, and firmly closing his eyes.

EE Blythe

December 18

The Week Before Christmas

'Twas the week before Christmas and all through the house uncertainty hung in the air with the decorations. Not that there were many decorations. In fact, the only Christmassy decoration was a vase filled with tall red and silver glittery sprays and branches of blossom that lit up when someone bothered to switch them on. It had been by the dining-room fireplace since 2015, because it was too cumbersome to put in storage, and because they liked it.

As each year passed it became an increasing chore to go up the steep attic stairs to bring down the large box that contained plastic fir branches, berries, cones, fruit and seven or eight robins that lived on the mantelpiece until Twelfth Night. As for the 14-inch high Christmas tree, that had been lost four years ago, somewhere up there, refusing to come when called. This year, cards would have to suffice, until they grew tired of standing them up when the draught blew them over whenever someone opened the door.

This year was different. This year they didn't know whether they were staying or going. For years they had run away from all the fuss and bother that Christmas entails. Now they awaited the decree from on high. Would they be allowed to travel, to stay overnight, to go on a journey that was not absolutely necessary? Did they dare risk turning up at the station and being sent home again, chastised for breaking the rules?

And, let us be truthful, did they really want to go away, at their age? The packing, the carrying, the crush and anxiety of train and bus travel, an unnecessary journey before the final one?

Wendy Goulstone

December 19

Christmas On Mars

'Twas the week before Christmas but Oswald didn't care.

Christmases had been pretty much the same for thousands of millennia. Not much happened. Not much changed.

Oswald was a microbe buried deep in the subsoil of Mars. Frozen in ice. Frozen for all time.

But he didn't mind; occasionally he could send out a little electric pulse to his fellow microbes to check they were still there, and occasionally he'd get a quick electric pulse back so that was OK.

Of course it had all been different once. Warm waters and a blue reddish sun.

But hurly burly wasn't in it.

Different aquatic creatures striving to evolve.

It churned up his mud oasis no end.

So no regrets when his sun imploded and a permanent winter descended.

Life was so much simpler now. Simply a state of permanent suspension.

But yesterday things became different. Oswald wasn't certain but he'd detected an almighty prang coming from the surface.

And then a deathly silence.

Today a distinct whirling vibration edging closer. The Chinese Challenger Spacecraft had landed, and even now was drilling deep into the frozen tundra.

Hell's bells, thought Oswald, that's torn it.

Simon Grenville

December 20

Disaster Averted

'Twas the week before Christmas and Santa had broken his leg. He lay in bed sulking as Mrs Claus paced around angrily.

'I'm sorry, Mrs Claus,' Twinkle the elf said, quivering with both guilt and fear next to her.

The irony wasn't lost on Mrs Claus that this had all happened because the elves had decided to take a break, celebrating being well ahead of schedule. It was meant to be an innocent game of hide and seek. How was Twinkle to know, as he curled up behind workstation number seven, that Santa would walk in at that very moment and go flying over the top of him?

'We'll need to bring in extra elf power now,' Mrs Claus huffed. 'And I suppose, yet again, I'll have to go and do the present delivering. This is the fourth time!'

Santa hid under the duvet with shame.

'Right, Twinkle,' she instructed, 'get your best team together. I need a beard making. And this time I want the softest red velvet for my suit. Not that itchy stuff I had before.'

'Yes, Mrs Claus,' Twinkle said, before running off to get started.

It seemed Christmas was saved again, thanks to Mrs Claus.

What a woman.

Lindsay Woodward

December 21

They Say It Was Christmas

We heard about it first when they were talking in the garden. The missus was keen to go with them. She wanted to see the old place again as she was born there, too. So we set off, going with them along the road, him walking, her on a donkey for she was near her time.

Sometimes we went in front, knowing the way, following the movements of the sun, then the stars when dusk fell. It was a long journey. The donkey often stumbled on the rough road.

When we arrived there was nowhere for them to stay. Not that it mattered to us, we didn't mind where we slept. But they went from house to house. No chance. Every inn was full to overflowing. 'No room' on every tongue. Then an innkeeper's wife took pity on them, put them up in a stable. Nice and warm in there, with the donkey and an old ox breathing sweet breath. Me and the missus, we slipped in, too. They didn't mind. We kept very quiet so as not to disturb them.

Then about midnight we woke up with a flutter. There was this little cry, such a sweet little sound, no louder than the cheep of a chick peeping through a shell. My missus just loves that moment.

There was coming and going all night, such a flutter, folk rich and poor. We watched it all from our perch in the rafters.

Wendy Goulstone

December 22

Slay Bells

As the slay bells rang out across the darkening sky, announcing the imminent arrival of the slay ride, she promised herself this would be the last time she took charge. It was time for someone younger to be the hero – she was too old. And she'd had enough. They just didn't realise how much work was involved with all the organising and preparing. Yesterday she'd been out in the woods cutting branches of holly and mistletoe. The day had been cold and frosty and her fingers had felt as if they'd drop off. No-one appreciated the traditions any more. The youngsters didn't care if it was holly or not – any tree branches would do for them.

Still, everything was ready now. The slay bells were getting closer. Dressed in her thick leather coat and gloves, wearing sturdy leather boots, she went outside. They were lined up waiting for her, clutching their tree branches. Most had holly, she was pleased to see. Some looked nervous, shuffling their feet and glancing about. Their first solstice, no doubt. She gave her usual speech, reminding them that team work was the key.

The slay bells had stopped. One by one the Visitors silently arrived, their pale faces keen with hunger, their eyes glowing with excitement, dressed in their traditional red outfits. He was leading the others as in previous years. He smiled at her, licking his lips in anticipation. She recognised him, but why wouldn't she? He was her son.

They stared at each other for a moment, then the scene exploded into violence.

The Visitors rushed at her troops, hands curled into claws, but they held steady. She charged at the leader, her sharpened holly branch at the ready. He laughed and leapt aside, but she knew his tactics of old, and leapt to the side with him. His mouth opened in surprise as she thrust the holly stake into his chest. He looked down, shrugged and crumbled into dust. A howl went up from the Visitors and they retreated, leaving a trail of blood black against the snow and piles of ash.

The slay ride was over for the year. Her troops had acquitted themselves well; the number of Visitors had been greatly reduced, while she had only lost two of hers.

'Well done,' she said. 'You fought well. Now we celebrate.'

Her last winter solstice had been a success. The slay bells would not be sounding again this winter. She would let them enjoy their victory before starting to prepare for the summer solstice when the sunflowers bloomed and stalked across the land in search of warm blood.

Fran Neatherway

December 23

Christmas Traditions

Deck the halls with boughs of holly,
Fa la la la la, la la la la.

In days of yore, it was deemed unlucky to bring evergreen, the traditional Christmas decoration, into the house until Christmas Eve. So the father of the house was despatched, heedless of the weather, to buy a real fir tree. After supper, the family would sit around the fire and make decorations of coloured paper or foil. These days, more often than not, Dad is sent into the loft to find the artificial tree bought from Argos a couple of years earlier. In 1880, Woolworths was the first retailer to sell Christmas tree ornaments, which were, and still are, very popular.

Decorating Christmas trees, a German custom, began in 1841 when Prince Albert bought a fir tree from Germany for his wife, Queen Victoria, and their children. Christmas trees in Victorian times were decorated with candles to remind children of the stars in the sky when Jesus was born. Today, candles are considered a fire hazard and have been replaced by strings of coloured electric lights – more a reminder of the fairground than the sacred symbolisation of the Light of the World. In addition, we put an angel, or star, on top of the tree. The angel represents the angel who brought glad tidings of great joy to the shepherds in the field, the star symbolises the star of Bethlehem.

The tallest Christmas tree in Britain stood twenty-five metres and was in Trafalgar Square, London. This year is the seventieth anniversary of Oslo's Christmas tree gift to London. The Norwegian spruce is the city of Oslo's gift to the people of Britain for the help and support they gave Norway during the Second World War.

The giving and receiving of gifts on Christmas Day morning also dates to Victorian times. Before then, gifts were exchanged on New Year's Day or Twelfth Night.

Father Christmas, or Santa Claus, is an ancestor of a pagan spirit who regularly appears in medieval mummer's plays. Olde Father Christmas was portrayed wearing long green robes with sprigs of holly in his long white hair. Children wrote letters telling him what they wanted at Christmas and then tossed them into the fire. The draft carried the letter up the chimney, and theoretically, Father Christmas read the smoke.

When I was a child, I wrote a letter to Father Christmas. I posted it in the red pillar box on the corner of our street. I had a reply from Lapland. It was an organisation set up by the Royal Mail that replied, but don't tell any small people in your family, as it will spoil their fun. It was a lovely idea and proved to my doubting school friends that just because we can't see someone doesn't mean they're not there.

Singing carols at Christmas is an English custom. In the Middle Ages, groups of serenades called 'waits' travelled from house to house, singing ancient carols and spreading the holiday spirit. The word 'carol' means 'song of joy'. Most of the carols we sing today were written in the nineteenth century.

The tradition of hanging stockings from the mantelpiece is because Father Christmas once dropped some gold coins while coming down the chimney. The coins would have been lost in the ashes if they hadn't fallen into a stocking hanging up to dry. Since then, on Christmas Eve, children hang up stockings, hoping to find them filled with gifts when they get up on Christmas morning.

Hanging holly and ivy was done to lift our spirits and remind us that spring was on its way. The custom of kissing under the mistletoe is descended from ancient Druid rites, and the tradition of raising a glass to wish someone good health comes from the Anglo-Saxon phrase waes hael, which means 'good health'. Like many ancient customs, it came about because a beautiful Saxon maiden named Rowena presented Prince Vortigen with a bowl of wine and toasted him with the words: 'Waes hael'.

Boxing Day, or the feast of Saint Stephen on December 26th, began in the mid-nineteenth century and is unique to the UK. Traditionally, on Boxing Day, alms boxes in English Churches were opened and the contents distributed among the poor. Servants were given the day off, and working people broke open their tip boxes. 'Boxing Day' was designated as the day the rich gave to the poor.

Could Dickens' book *A Ghost Story of Christmas*, better known as *A Christmas Carol*, have influenced the rich to give to the poor? It was written during a decline in Christmas traditions, and the story reminded people of the importance of Christmas. It also deals with two of Dickens' recurrent themes: social injustice and poverty, and their causes and effects. It was published the week before Christmas in 1843 and sold more than six thousand copies in the first week, so you never know.

Madalyn Morgan

December 24

Christmas Eve 2020

On Christmas Eve, Jenny lay awake, terrified Father Christmas would come down the chimney into her bedroom. Granny had told her that's how Father Christmas delivered presents to all the good little children. Granny's house was old and made lots of scary noises at night.

Jenny had met Father Christmas once, in his grotto. She'd screamed and burst into tears and run away from the scary white-bearded giant in the red suit. She'd been too afraid to sleep in case he came into her bedroom. So Daddy went outside to collect her presents from Father Christmas as soon as he heard the sleigh bells. That's what daddies did. And he did that every year.

This Christmas was going to be different. Mummy and Jenny were staying at Granny's house, "to look after her". Daddy wasn't here. He was at the hospital, helping poorly people get better. Jenny talked to him on Mummy's laptop, but it wasn't the same. Mummy was sad. She said it was to keep them all safe. Jenny wanted to be kept safe from Father Christmas.

Granny was nice and she made lovely cakes, but Jenny had to be quiet and tidy, and she couldn't watch her television. She wanted to go home, where she felt safe, where her friends were. She even wanted to go to school.

When Mummy came to put her to bed, Jenny could see that she had been crying.

'When's Daddy coming back?' she asked.

'I don't know,' Mummy said. 'Soon, I hope.'

Jenny hoped so too. She snuggled under the bedclothes and tried to go to sleep.

+ +

She woke up when she heard the footsteps, big, heavy footsteps coming up the stairs. It wasn't Mummy or Granny. The steps were too heavy for Granny and too loud for Mummy. Jenny was too scared to move. She hid under the duvet and pulled the bedclothes over her head, leaving a tiny gap to peer through.

The footsteps paused at the top of the stairs, then walked across the landing and stopped again outside her bedroom door. The door creaked open. Jenny peeped and saw a man carrying a big sack.

She screamed. 'Mummy, Mummy, it's Father Christmas, Mummy!'

The lights went on. There was Daddy, putting a bag of presents at the foot of her bed. Mummy and Granny were there too. Daddy picked up Jenny and hugged her. She flung her arms round his neck, and hugged him tight.

'Two vaccinations and two negative tests,' he said. 'Back to bed, sweetheart. I'll see you in the morning.'

'Daddy, Daddy, you came!' Jenny was so happy she could barely speak.

'Of course I did,' Daddy said. 'Someone had to go and meet Father Christmas and collect your presents.'

Jenny fell asleep immediately.

Fran Neatherway

December 25

Father Christmas

Smart and suited Steve stood at the sink in the small and messy office kitchen. He was filling the kettle with water while singing to himself: 'Do you believe in Father Christmas?'

Sally, a tall, well-dressed woman, entered the kitchen with her bright red mug in hand.

'It's *I believe in Father Christmas*, you idiot,' she stated as she smacked down her mug on the side.

'I see your usual jovial self is embracing this most wonderful time of year again,' Steve said, flicking the kettle on.

'How can I be happy? It's Christmas Eve and I'm stuck here with you. I'd rather be anywhere but here.'

'Like two thousand miles away?' Steve asked, a slight smirk on his lips.

'Stop it.'

'Perhaps driving home for Christmas?'

'I'm warning you, stop it. Or it will be your chestnuts roasting on an open fire.'

'Ooh, someone's Frosty the Snowman.'

'You know I have no patience for your silly little games.'

'But it's beginning to look a lot like Christmas,' Steve said as he casually grabbed the milk from the fridge.

'If you don't stop it, this will be your last Christmas.'

Steve placed the milk on the side and pretended to look confused. 'I can't stop if you play along.'

'What?'

'Go on, stay another day. You'll be rocking around the Christmas tree before you know it.'

Sally scowled at Steve as the kettle reached its bubbling finale. Steve loved these games. It was so easy to wind the office monster up.

Steve made his coffee, and when he'd placed down his teaspoon, he raised his mug.

'Happy Christmas, war is over?' he offered. It was Christmas after all.

'Let it snow!' Sally snapped back in reply. She whacked her teaspoon down and stormed out of the kitchen, leaving Steve laughing behind.

Lindsay Woodward

December 26

Mince Pies

It was the night before Christmas when I saw it. I took the biscuits out of the kitchen cupboard and there it was, a small grey mouse nibbling away, with crumbs everywhere.

'Oi!' I shouted. It shot off under the fridge.

Fetching the cat, I carried him into the kitchen. 'Basil,' I told him firmly, 'you have a job to do tonight.' He didn't look at all pleased. I put down a saucer of milk. It was nature after all, I told myself - nothing to worry about.

But I still lay awake in bed an hour later. Had I really set Basil up to commit a murder on Christmas Eve? Back to the kitchen I went, opened the door gingerly. The first thing I saw by moonlight were two shapes on the counter. One, I realised, was the turkey. The other, Basil, chewing.

'Oi!' I shouted. He shot off.

I switched on the light. 'Basil, how could you?' I cried.

But he miaowed at me, 'How could you?!' he seemed to say.

And the mouse? I switched the light off again and stood perfectly still. A rustling started up in the cupboard. Basil's eyes lit-up.

There it was! It had started on the mince pies!

Theresa Le Flem

December 27

Snow

Snow. Snowflakes falling, dancing in the streetlights, happy to meet their ends on roofs or gardens, cars or roads. Trees stark against the pale sky, its peculiarly light colour reflecting back from the bleached earth. Branches dripping ice, reaching up into the chilly night.

Silence blankets everything. Coldness cuts through the thick air. Snow crunches under foot with a satisfying sound, muffled as if under water.

The church spire, tall and dark against the sky, points to heaven. Frost on the windows creates icons of snowflakes, each one different. Light spills out, forming patterns on the white covered churchyard. Grey snow-capped teeth rear up, bearing messages: In Loving Memory; Rest in Peace.

Voices lift up in song, joyous melodies of good tidings, and breach the silence of the snow. Bells ring, celebrating the new-born, welcoming the child.

People walking home, hands in pockets against the cold, scarves wound tight, heads thrust forward, cheerful excited voices, ignoring the cold, eagerly anticipating the morning.

Everything is silent once more. Still the snowflakes tumble down, piling deeper and deeper. And far above the snow, where the night sky is navy dark, a lone star shines steadily bright.

Fran Neatherway

On a Christmas Eve many years ago, I went to Midnight Mass in a tiny Norman church in a village near where I grew up. When I left the church, it had started to snow and it was magical.

December 28

Wonderful Christmas Time

I light a candle to our love, with love all problems disappear...

A long time ago in the village of East Manley there had been a lot of complaints about last year's Christmas Fayre: too commercial, too many people selling their craft ideas from all over the county, no fun stalls and no carols, no big surprises.

Nice Nick, the vicar, felt so isolated by these unkind comments. In the church, alone, he addressed his dog, "Jet, I thought the only lonely place was on the moon." Christmas loomed.

Perhaps he could cross music off the list.

The Saint Denys' School Choir did their best but struggled. Their frog chorus just managed to make a noise like a bell but Nick felt he should try to involve them somehow so musical presentation was indicated.

Then the brainwave. Mr and Mrs Allerton developed their circus skills after retiring and Nick imagined an amusing Santa clown act to surprise the children; little did he know they had moved on to more difficult tricks.

He had an idea who could open the fayre. The arrangements were straightforward. Nick knew Dave who knew Mike who was James' brother. James was younger then and loved to be invited to real life events with Linda.

+ +

The big day arrived and a small crowd gathered in the sports field next to the church. He started to see the ten metre towers newly erected by scaffolders in the field adjacent to the church. Nick saw the Allertons and waved. "Should be some great clowning tonight!" He laughed, misunderstanding completely. He also completely missed the puzzled expressions on the faces of the circus obsessed couple.

The hired bench seating looked reasonably safe. Nick was happy that the Allertons were as ready as they would ever be; happy the church choir was strictly amateur and the choir master had limited their contribution as far as possible to merely *ding dong ding dong* with an optimistic occasional *oo oo oo oo oo ooooo!*

Finally the guest of honour Sir James and Linda, toast of 1979, music business walked down casually from the local The Fountain.

To be fair, the Christmas pipers and Michael Jackson tributes left all a little cold.

Finally the main attraction, John and Cynthia Allerton: tightrope walkers extraordinaire. A large crowd had been drawn from all over the county and was about to hold their breath at the now 40m line looking rather intimidating. John on one pylon and Cynthia on the other walked gingerly simultaneously to the middle but what were the strange objects they held? Not quite the same as normal balance aids. They were approaching the midpoint.

The crowd could clearly see now, folding out from their hands, a chair each and from John a table, from Cynthia a wine bottle and from nowhere two glasses. With insane levels of skill, they placed the chairs and the table on the line and proceeded to have the most extraordinary date night in front of a really impressed audience. Momentarily, Cynthia's nerve appeared to go as a glass tumbler dropped the 30 feet to be caught deftly by Sir James.

John shouted at Cynthia

Raise a glass and don't look down.

We're simply having a wonderful Christmas time

The audience seemed to join in with the chant.

The couple shared the drink and quietly returned to their pylons with no further incident.

Nick accosted Sir James at the end of the performance. "What did you think Sir James? Was it worth the journey?"

"Absolutely staggered. Are you sure those two are amateurs? I'm definitely going to write about this."

Chris Wright

December 29

The Festive Spirit

She finished her prayers to the gods and snuggled into the warmth of her bed. It had gotten dark early on this the longest night of the year. She had stayed up later than normal to help her mother adorn the house with holly leaves atop the doors and windows. It was a silly tradition, she thought as she lay in the dark of her room. The holly was said to drive away the dark spirits that roamed the land on this solstice night, hunting for naughty children to take away to the spirit realm. Upon finding their children still in bed the next morning the adults would celebrate all day with sweet cakes and the giving of presents and dancing and a great village feast come the end of the day.

In her twelve years she had never once glimpsed a sight of one of these spirits, nor had heard of any child ever going missing after this night, and she knew a few of the boys and Lisa the Smith's daughter were particularly naughty. She always tried to be good, but had she been good enough? She chided herself for thinking such childish nonsense, the spirits weren't real. She eventually drifted to sleep.

A clatter of wood and a deepening chill in the room awoke her. She lay in bed with her eyes still closed, it was nothing she told herself and willed herself to return to sleep. Then she heard the distinct creak of the floor. Was something in the room with her? Another creak of the wooden floor and a clickety clack that made her think of claws. No, she said mentally to herself, the spirits can't be real. Clickety clack, clickety clack went the claws on the wooden floor. The room was getting steadily colder and she wanted to curl up to get warmer but at the same time she did not want the spirit to know she was awake. Stop it, she said to herself, the spirits can't be real. But then the clickety clack, clickety clack, clickety clack upon the wooden floor.

She lay completely still, not daring to move an inch and hardly breathing, hoping it would think she was asleep. Clickety clack. And then she only just managed to stifle a scream as she felt its needle thin claws scratchily caress her cheek. A voice like a hive of angry bees seemed to whisper in her ears, "I know when you are sleeping, I know when you are awake!" The claws seemed to dig deeper for a second and the voice sounded again. "But have you been bad or good?"

She wanted to scream for her mother. She wanted to fight against this thing that had her face but the dread fear she was feeling held her fast. There was a deep inhaling as if it was trying to pick up some scent from her.

Again the voice spoke but this time it was edged with a deep disappointment. "Good." Then the claws immediately left her face. Clickety clack. There was a bang from across the room and she sat up with a scream. Clickety clack.

Her mother came bursting into the room with a lit candle dispelling the darkness and the girl looked around.

"The spirit was here!" she said

But looking over at the window, she saw the wooden shutters had been blown open and the lifeless branch of the apple tree was being buffeted against the wood of the window. Clickety clack. She touched her face where the spirit had touched her and she looked at the floor and a smaller branch had been blown off the tree and fully into her room.

"Oh you poor dear, look, it's just the tree. There are no spirits in here, we hung up the holly remember? Now chuck out that branch, close the window and go back to sleep pet."

"Yes, Ma." The girl obeyed her mother and got out of bed and picked up the branch. Had it really just been this that had blown onto her bed? But what about the voice? Had that been her imagination? It must have been. There were no such things as spirits she told herself as she crossed the room and tossed the branch out of the window. Besides her mother was right, even if they did exist, they had placed holly above each door and window. She poked her head outside and looked above the window but there was no sprig of holly hanging there. Looking around in a panic, she spotted it lying on the ground. The wind must have blown it off.

Closing the wooden shutters, she climbed back into the bed and her mother left her once more in the dark. She had no doubt now, she had been visited by the spirit. Its bee-like voice echoing in her mind. "Good." Knowing that, she smiled content in the knowledge she would not be taken this year and curling up beneath the blankets was soon fast asleep once more.

Christopher Trezise

December 30

The Snowflake Makers

It was winter season. There was ice but no snow. Where was the snow? In that time, snow hadn't been created yet. Yes, snow was created. Snow was made by a man by the name of Evander Lour. He wondered why the winter was so plain. Leaves turned orange and bronze in Autumn, flowers would grow and bloom in the spring, but nothing ever happened in the winter. Yes, it got colder. A lake, or two, would freeze up, and animals would go into hibernation, but winter didn't have much to offer. What could Evander Lour create that would make winter special?

Evander went to his daughter, Eris', room. As he opened the door, Eris' dark eyes gave him a blank stare.

"What are you doing in my room, Dad?" Eris spat. Her jet-black hair sparkled in the light, reflecting from her window.

"I have an idea." Evander spoke with a smile.

"You always have ideas, and they have always failed. Get out!" Eris shouted as she slammed the bedroom door.

Evander waited at her door for a few minutes before letting out a small sigh and leaving the hall. He headed towards his study. It wasn't a considerably large room, but it was perfect for him. He sat down at the wooden desk and began to scribble his latest plan on parchment.

+ +

A six-sided shape had formed on Evander's page. It was hexagonal, but it had arms coming from it with lines and a swirling designed on it. Evander had designed his perfect snowflake. It was late, but he didn't mind. He had to show his daughter his creation. He almost skipped to his daughter's door and knocked on it lightly.

"Eris, are you awake?" Evander said in a whispered tone. He heard some rustling coming from his daughter's room, and then he watched as the door in front of him swung open.

"Dad," Eris said. "What's up?" Her makeup made her look tired as she gave him a neutral look.

"I have a new drawing. Would you like to see it?" Evander's eyes looked sad. He had not seen his teenage daughter for a few hours, and he felt miserable. Eris looked at the parchment in her father's hand, and she turned her head to the left.

"Come in," she directed. Evander slowly crept into her room and headed for her black desk. Eris looked at it for a moment.

"What is it meant to be, Dad?" she questioned.

Evander looked at her. "It's called a snowflake." They both stared at the page for a second.

"A snowflake? What does it do?" Eris wondered.

Evander stopped to think for a moment. "It is meant to fall from the sky, stick on the ground and bring joy to adults and children." He smiled for a moment before he watched his daughter turn to him.

"How do we make it, Dad?" Eris smiled faintly.

"You really want to?" Evander asked. He watched Eris nod.

"Yes Dad, we haven't made anything together since Mum died." She grabbed the parchment drawing from her desk and proceeded to leave her small bedroom. "Come on, Dad," Eris said as she walked to her Father's study, "let's make our snowflake." She smiled at her Dad.

+ +

Evander grated ice until it was in oddly shaped pieces. They began to fill the parchment snowflake design with ice pieces until the snowflake was formed. Eris and Evander looked at each other and smiled.

"How are we able to make all of these pieces stay together?" Eris questioned.

Evander put his rubber-glove-covered hand on his chin. "Let's leave it to melt a little and then put it into the freezer for a few hours so it all sticks together," he suggested.

Eris picked up the ice sculpture and headed towards the freezer, her Father opened it for her, and she placed it in. She shut the lid and turned to Evander.

"I am sorry, Dad. Sorry, I haven't been around here much. Mum's passing has really had an effect on me." Eris' eyes were full of sadness and sorrow.

Evander looked at his daughter and could see her sadness. "Eris, it's okay. I know you miss Mum." His words sounded sincere as he took Eris into a small hug.

+ +

Evander had slept in his study. His eyelids felt heavy as he tried so hard to open them. Eventually, his body left his chair and headed towards the freezer. He opened it to reveal a perfectly symmetrical shape. His snowflake had worked.

"Eris! Eris!" Evander shouted with desperation. He heard footsteps from his teenage daughter as she raced to his study.

Eris huffed. "Dad? What's wrong?"

Evander looked at her and suddenly smiled. "It worked. Our snowflake worked." Both of them began to dance, a dance to celebrate Evander's first successful invention.

"Dad, you did it!" Eris said, her face beaming with a smile. "How are you going to manufacture this? And what's going to happen when it melts?" Eris then questioned.

Evander thought to himself for a small moment, "Manufacturing: we can make it tiny, very tiny, tiny enough for a magnifying glass."

Eris looked at him. "And what about melting, Dad? Because it will melt." Evander did not need to think about his answer. He knew what he was going to say. "Just let it melt. If the temperature is cold enough, it'll turn into snow, and when it gets warm, obviously, it will melt." Evander then took his snowflake into the hall and put on his coat. "You coming?" He asked.

Eris ran and put on her black coat to match her outfit and hair colour. "Where are we going?" Eris asked.

"I am going to the council. We need to get workers to manufacture tiny snowflakes." Evander and Eris left their house and made their way to the Councillor's office.

\+   \+

"Excuse me?" The Councillor spoke. Evander and Eris were sat opposite the Councillor. The snowflake was staring at him on his desk.

"We need workers to make snowflakes." Evander looked at him.

"How many?" the Councillor asked.

"About twenty or so," Eris interrupted. The Councillor and Evander looked at her for a small moment before Evander turned back to meet the Councillor's eyes.

"Yeah, like she said, at least twenty, maybe more. Depends on how long it takes to make them." Evander folded his arms.

"Okay, well, I can't just give you workers. You will need volunteers," the Councillor suggested.

Evander nodded. "Volunteers, okay." He then left the Councillor's office with Eris tailing behind him.

"Dad, what're you thinking?" she questioned.

"I am going to turn the house into a mini snowflake factory and hire some workers who need jobs," he explained as he rushed back, with Eris, to his home.

\+   \+

Evander and Eris turned their house into a working snowflake-making factory. They had hired three people to help them create their miniature sculptures. The process was long because of the snowflakes' size, but before the day was over, they had made 45 mini snowflakes. Evander was pleased about his creation. However, he had a small problem. How was he going to let it snow?

"We need planes." Evander raised his voice to his daughter.

"Why do we need planes for?" Eris questioned.

"We need planes so we can chuck buckets of snowflakes out, so it looks like it's raining. Eris, we need the wow-factor. We need winter to be a memorable season," Evander told her. He headed into a room that used to be his kitchen and headed towards a red-haired man.

"Ned, we need to borrow your plane," Evander told him. Ned gave Evander a dirty gaze but silently chucked him the keys.

"I would not give to ye if u weren't payin' ma bills," Ned told him.

+ +

The trolley full of snowflakes was loaded onto the plane.

"When I press the button, tip one basket and release the snowflakes," Evander told Eris. Without a word, she nodded and headed into the back of the plane, Evander up front. He turned on the ignition and prepared himself for flight. The cool winter air was thin, the sky was cloudy, and white. Evander looked down at the world beneath him and pressed his thumb onto the button.

"Now!" Evander shouted. Eris tipped the first basket out and released the snowflakes into the world. The flakes flurried downwards as Evander watched people leave their homes to watch the strange flakes flutter past them.

+ +

The people on the ground were in awe of the cold, shimmering flakes that were floating around them.

"What is this?" one lady asked. Smiles were suddenly seen on their faces. The flakes formed on the ground beneath them into a crunchy layer of white snow. The people did not know how to react. This was a new sight for them. A young boy reached down to pick up the snow, and he formed it into a small ball. He threw it at his friend, who then picked up a snowball and threw it back. They finally had something to remember winter by.

Since then, Evander would come out every winter and release snowflakes into the world. His daughter, Eris, took over the snowflake business when her father died, and she passed the snowflake trade down to her two sons.

My name is Cecille Morgan, and I am the Great-Granddaughter of Evander Lour. I currently own the snowflake business, and every year, I go out in my plane and drop snowflakes into the world to have people remember winter as being full of happiness, friendship, and laughter.

Chloe Huntington

December 31
Blue, With Stars

He'd been on his own for Christmas. The others had gone, but not him. So he'd stayed put, alone. 'It's because I'm damaged,' he said to himself, looking at the white plaster. He'd overheard someone once say that he was unsafe – that's why he'd ended up homeless for a while, separated from the others for some weeks. He was back with the others now, and they were all in a new home. He had hoped this Christmas would be different: parties, people, jelly, cake, children; but although there was plenty of noise, and laughter, he still felt separate, and now alone.

And lonely.

The view wasn't bad. Not the tidiest of bedrooms, maybe, but comfortable, and now the big wardrobe had gone and things had moved round a bit, he was nicely secure, with a view through the window of the street below, if he wanted to look. He didn't. He looked at the light cover of dust all around him, and felt rather neglected.

And alone.

It wasn't Christmas now, that had been and gone, and he'd heard the laughter in the street on New Year's Eve as everyone shouted 'Happy New Year', and shook hands with strangers, saying this next year just had to be better than the old one. Oh yeah?

Since then there'd been a sort of anti-climax. The street was empty in the day as the great return to work had happened. Everyone coming home at tea-time, tired and cold, as the weather turned. Grumbles about late buses, or non-appearing buses and missed connections. Grumbles about eating Christmas leftovers, from the freezer.

Again.

He knew when the Christmas tree, and the decorations in the hallway, had all been taken down, and the baubles and lights had been safely put away ready for next year, but he hadn't seen one of them. Not once. Just heard the swearing as the ground floor of the house had been returned to normal. He'd missed it all.

He'd just stayed put!

But this day was different. It had started quiet and bright, and someone had said the word snow. Somehow it had lifted the atmosphere in the house. And he'd been lifted too.

Physically.

Finally, he got to see the kitchen! Just as much of a muddle as the bedroom, even down to the dust on the higher shelves, but warm and friendly. And there were all the others, at the table.

Waiting for him.

But first, he was settled in by the cooker, where all the light from the window fell on him, and he could see the garden, with the snow-dressed trees and bushes, and the grey sky showing blue patches, where the sunlight cut through to make everything twinkle and sparkle.

It certainly raised spirits.

Suddenly he was being stroked, and something cold was being spread over the bare plaster. With a bit of a shock he realised someone cared about him. The bare plaster was now blue, not quite the same blue as the rest of him, but close enough so that he didn't stand out as damaged.

Or unsafe.

'There,' she said, turning back from rinsing the brush under the tap. 'Not as good as new, but returned to the land of the living.'

And later, he was wrapped in tissue, and put with the others into the 'Best Crocks' basket, ready to be used on the next Special Occasion.

Not unsafe.

Not damaged.

Not alone.

Not lonely.

EE Blythe

A Story for Every Day of Winter

January

A Story for Every Day of Winter

January 1st

This Year

This year I shall get a rescue dog.

This year I shall learn to play the piano.

This year I shall conduct a survey of hedgehogs in our garden throughout the year.

This year I shall become an ordinand in training, and I shall study hard, and I shall hate it.

This year I shall marry a beautiful fifty-year-old woman, and we will live together and make our home together and sleep together, and we will have no children.

On further thought, cross out "beautiful" and substitute "talented".

This year I shall write a computer game, and it will be extraordinarily successful, and people will complain on social media that it did not win an award.

This year I shall make a major breakthrough in mathematics and prove Alan Turing and Alonzo Church wrong—ha-ha!—and become a Fellow of the Royal Society.

This year I shall carry on going to the Rugby Café Writers, and go to church, and continue to participate in the u3a, and look after my mother. In the years after, I shall dwindle and go to my grave.

Jim Hicks

January 2nd

A New Beginning

So far, so good. As Chief Medical Officer aboard Pioneer 37 of the Scatterseed mission, it was planned that I would be the first to be roused. And here I am, awake and fully functioning it would seem, but totally alone on just one of the vast hibernation decks. Soon I shall begin the re-awakening process, starting with the full medical team, who will then oversee bringing the 5,000 migrants on board back to life. But for now, I will allow myself a short, solitary reflection on the planet I used to call home.

How did we reach the point where, not only human life, but nearly all plant and animal life became unsustainable? Why did we not heed decades of warnings? Why did we ignore and often dismiss growing evidence as our environment degraded at an ever increasing pace? Of course, over the latter part of what we knew as the 21st century, there was increasing concern, then desperation, and finally mass panic and chaos. But we had left it all too late.

This was not due to a lack of ingenuity, or technology, or even finance; no, our failure was the inability to co-operate, to reach out, to consider others. Humankind polarised, fragmented. We built walls, formed pacts, harboured false suspicion, hurling accusations at opposing alliances. And those who were powerful and wealthy enough began to plan their escape. Thousands and thousands of pioneering explorers would seek out and inhabit new worlds. Or was this tiny percentage of the human population just another group of desperate refugees? From the dawning of the 22nd century, fleets of huge inter-galactic life-rafts, fifty from the Western Democratic Alliance alone, were abandoning Mother Earth.

Such a sad and desperate plan. Many of the first escaping craft were shot down by enemy missiles before they had even left Earth's atmosphere. And doubtless, many more are marooned in the vast, unknown and lonely cosmos, never reaching their intended destinations. And what of the millions who were left on the dying Earth? Thankfully, we will never know their hellish fate.

Pioneer 37 is now orbiting Exo-planet 4398z, seven light years from Earth. The universe has been seeded; the human species is desperately seeking a second chance. For me, one question remains, lurking in the dark, shadowy recesses of my conscience: are we even deserving of a new beginning?

Steve Redshaw

January 3rd

A Christmas Character

I lie here on my back in absolute darkness. If I try to stand up I know my head will meet the lid, and I cannot move my arms sideways without soon feeling the walls of my narrow box. So I lie and I wait. Not long now.

It starts with a movement, and the lid will be lifted. A hand will gently raise me into the light and stroke my golden hair. My dress will be smoothed out, its tinsel trim examined for tarnish and my wand reunited with my hand. Soon I shall be placed again right at The Top. Below me the lametta will gently wave and glitter. I shall be set above the mock candles. Real ones were banned after a tiny fire in 2017. They thought it was caused by the wind, but Caliban the Cat and I knew otherwise.

The pretty lights will be arranged to display my best features, and I shall be up there, above the ancient wooden angel, and the modern glass Santa, and as long as I'm nowhere near that interminably grinning Clown, I'll be a happy fairy. Every year he announces he's the oldest ornament on the tree. I ask you!

Sadly he's always been out of the reach of any cat, even Ginger who once brought us all toppling down. Our clown just laughed and shouted, "Timber!"

I had to use my wings in a hurry, I can tell you, but I made a safe landing on top of the TV. Luckily the tree had lodged itself against the sofa, thanks to a quick wave of my wand, so we all survived intact.

I'm looking forward to our annual reunion. Soon I shall shimmer; soon I shall dazzle. I shall play my small part in the magic of Christmas.

Chris Rowe

January 4th

What Do You Mean, I Can't Come?

I knew something was up with her the minute she arrived. She was bristly and off, slamming stuff about as she put my shopping away, huffing to herself while she was cooking and the like, but I took no notice; that's just our Jess.

When I'd finished my tea she stood herself in front of me and announced,

'Mum, I need a holiday.'

'Ooh no!' I said, 'it's too cold. And anyway, Christmas is coming. I've got stuff to do.'

'I don't mean with you, Mum,' she bristled. 'I mean me, Steve, and the kids. I need to get away. I'm exhausted.'

'Exhausted!' I'll admit I was a bit surprised by that. 'What am I supposed to do?' I said. 'And what about school? You can't take the kids out of school.'

'It's half term soon and you've got loads of time to do your Christmas stuff. Don't worry, I've found a lovely place for you, just while we're gone. You'll like it.'

'Oh no, you don't! I'm not going into any home.'

'It's respite care. It's only for a few weeks.'

'Respite? I don't need respite!'

'No, Mum. I do. I'm at the end of my tether and I need a break. We both need a change of scenery and it might help you move on.'

'Move on from what?'

'Dad.'

'I don't want to move on from your dad. I don't want a change of scenery; I've got everything I want here. Why can't you just take some time off work if you're that tired? Tell Steve and the kids to pull their fingers out.'

'No, Mum. You rely totally on me and won't let anyone else in to help and I'm tired.'

'You're my daughter, it's what daughters do.'

'Not to the point of making them ill, it isn't. I hoped you'd be reasonable. I should have known you'd play up…as usual.' Then she burst into tears and stormed out.

+ +

I should have been the one crying, not her. She only works in an office; it's not exactly hard work, is it? And the kids are nearly teenagers for heaven's sake! I know I struggle now Joe's gone but I've got my pride and like I said, that's what families are for. When Jess was growing up, I was always on the go, not sat on my backside all day pressing buttons on a computer. And on top of all that I looked after my mam and she could be a right cantankerous old devil. But it was the right thing to do.

A bit later Jess phoned me to see how I was, then she got upset again and started blubbering but no matter how I tried to reason with her she wouldn't budge. She said she needed a break and that was that. I asked her if she was divorcing me like she did Peter and she told me not to be so silly.

'If your dad was here you wouldn't be shoving me off somewhere strange,' I said.

'If Dad was here I wouldn't have to,' she bit back, 'because when he was here you coped just fine.'

'What the hell do you want me to do?' I yelled, 'You know I've never been able to cope on my own. I'm too old to learn now.'

'For heaven's sake, Mum, you're seventy two! You're not even old yet!'

'Easy for you to say when you're in your prime, isn't it. Your day will come.'

'Mum! I'm fifty years old, for God's sake!' she yelled. Then she hung up on me.

So I got packed off to the home, the dog was sent to kennels and they buggered off to Lanzarote.

+ +

I spent the first day sitting in a chair against the wall, looking at old people sitting in chairs against the walls looking at me. The next day I refused to come out of my room. I told them if I had to be here then I'd rather look out of my bedroom window than watch people sitting around like zombies. At least I could see some life out of there, the birds flitting about and the trees blowing and that. There was a woman with three little kiddies waiting for the school bus at the stop across the road. Busy little bees they were, jumping and hopping about. The little one seemed hell bent on jumping under a car; she'd got her work cut out with them, I can tell you! It took me back to when me and Jess used to get the bus to and from school every day. I hated it. It either was too hot, too cold, or too crowded; it was a proper trial really. I wanted to learn to drive but Joe said I didn't need to drive because he could take us everywhere. He wasn't around for the school run though. Or when I had to carry heavy bags of shopping, but there was no moving him. Jess has the same stubborn streak.

+ +

After a few days I realised that not everyone sat around staring into space. Some days it was like Piccadilly Circus with the number of people passing my door. I was dying to know where they went, so one day I asked Amira. She's lovely and always made a point of chatting with me while tidying round, which is more than anyone else did. She said that she'd get Rachel, the activities co-ordinator to talk to me, because there's always something going on for those who wanted to take part. I wasn't sure I wanted to take part in anything. I just wanted to know what was going on.

Rachel came to see me the next morning. She was only young but she was lovely. She said they did all sorts of things like arts and crafts, singing, and even line dancing if I was interested. If she'd said basket weaving I would have shown her the door, but she didn't. She said they have days out too when the weather's fine and they were hoping to go to the coast the next day. That got my interest. I haven't been to the seaside for ages. Rachel said she wasn't sure I was ready for that. She said she knew my history and how anxious I get if I'm outside the house, and as I hadn't been very mobile of late, maybe I should do one of the indoor activities first. That really pushed me over the edge, that did. It was the last straw really.

'What do you mean I can't come!' I said. 'I can do anything if I want to, I just haven't felt like doing much lately.' I was so cross my eyes started to water. 'Nobody wants me to go anywhere. Our Jess has buggered off on holiday without me and now you won't even let me go to the seaside!'

I think Rachel was a bit taken aback but she said she would talk to the manager and maybe just me and her could go out another day, but she might take a wheelchair along, just in case. Cheeky mare, wheelchair indeed! I kept my cool; she was only trying to help, but I'd be damned if I was going in a wheelchair!

+ +

The next day I was chatting with Amira and it turns out that she lives a few streets away from my house, although I've never seen her out and about; but then I don't suppose I would, seeing as I don't go out. Her Mum's a widow too and she's the same age as me, and lives with Amira and her family. I told her that her mum's lucky she has a daughter who will look after her, and Amira laughed and said it was the opposite really. Apparently her mum's always been fiercely independent. She does most of the cooking and odd bits around the house, when she has time, which actually isn't all that often because she's always off out to clubs and coffee mornings and such like. I was a bit taken aback to be honest, what with her being on her own and that. I said as much to Amira and got a proper funny look in return.

'What do you mean, Joan? Don't you think you should have a life now your husband's gone?'

'No. It's not that. It's just that my Joe took care of the running of the house, the money, and stuff. He said he didn't want me worrying my pretty head over bills and nonsense and I should just concentrate on keeping house and looking after him and Jess. He proper spoiled me, he did.'

'Ok... I see... But now you're alone you've proved you can do it, haven't you?'

'I wouldn't have a clue to be honest. Jess deals with my money and pays my bills and stuff. I don't know what I'd do without her.'

'Don't you go out shopping or for coffee?'

'I haven't been out like that since Joe died. I get a bit panicky without him to back me up.'

Next thing I knew I was being hugged so tight it made my eyes water and my ring got caught in Amira's cardigan and I couldn't let go. I haven't had a hug for such a long time.

Anyway, I had a think about what Amira said and a couple of mornings later I plucked up the courage to go to arts and crafts. Everyone was very nice and I really enjoyed it. It brought back memories of when I was at school. I'd been good at art then but I'd forgotten. Kay, who runs the group, also does classes in the guild-house in town two afternoons a week. She said I would be welcome to go along once I'm back home. I said I'd think about it but I didn't think I would really.

A few days later Rachel persuaded me to give the musical movement session a try. I resisted at first because I haven't really done much exercise the last few years and my old bones have stiffened up something chronic, but she wouldn't take no for an answer and said I could do it sitting in a chair. So I gave it a go and boy, did I feel better afterwards. Rachel was impressed with me too and gave me some exercises to do every day. She said by the time I went home I'd be dancing round the room. I thought that was a bit ambitious of her but I admit I did feel quite good.

The best thing though was Amira told her mum about me and she decided she wanted to meet me. Her name's Jyoti but everyone calls her Joy and she really is a joy. We've become quite good friends.

+ +

So now it's three weeks later. I'm home and I feel like a new woman.

I've made plans to meet up with Joy next week. She's coming here for lunch then afterwards she's going to show me how to catch the bus into town and back and I'm going to start my Christmas shopping. I'm getting myself a mobile phone too, just a simple one. Joy says I'll be able to master it easy; then our Jess will be able to contact me if I'm out. It might stop her fretting. I've decided I'm going to join the art group too. I can always get a taxi if I get spooked with the bus.

I think Jess is a bit miffed with the new me. She had a think on holiday apparently and decided to work part-time for a while. Now she wants to come to art class with me. I told her absolutely not! She should get out and make her own friends, not be hanging around with me. We've all got our own lives to lead, after all.

Rosemary Marks

January 5

Relative Values

It was already dark and the shops were closing, spilling pools of yellow light on the glistening wet pavements. Sharon walked faster, heels beating an impatient tattoo, passing beneath the Christmas decorations hanging across the High Street, snowflakes and angels, stars and Santas all etched in twinkling fairy lights. They looked sad and bedraggled now. The store windows were full of unwanted stuff, red and white banners proclaiming: **New Year Sale Only 2 Days Left.**

Sharon didn't like the dark and she didn't like New Year. A fine drizzle coated her hair and her feet were wet. She shivered and pulled her coat tighter, wishing she'd worn more sensible shoes. Then she saw the man huddled in a doorway, a small, brown dog of indeterminate ancestry curled up beside him, tail wrapped around its body. She had noticed him earlier on the way to her appointment and had thought that there was something vaguely familiar about him. He was bundled up in several layers of old clothing, newspaper clearly visible underneath through the holes in his outermost garments. A fringe of lank, greasy hair stuck out beneath a bright red woolly bobble-hat pulled down tight over his ears.

Unaware of Sharon's gaze, he pulled a bottle out of his overcoat pocket and took a swig, wiping his mouth on the back of his hand before returning the bottle to its hiding place. She felt both pity and disgust as she watched him, but these emotions were superseded by embarrassment as he looked up and their eyes met. He grinned at her, revealing a mouth full of gaps and broken, discoloured teeth, his face drawn and grimy under patchy stubble. Sharon looked away immediately as the blood rushed to her face and she hurried off, only to hear him behind her.

'Oi, Missus, what you looking at?'

Sharon walked faster, scared by the note of aggression in his voice. He followed her and the dog pit-patted along beside him.

'Can you spare the price of a cup of tea, Missus?' he wheedled.

She ignored him.

'Stuck up cow!' he yelled at her back as he gave up and returned to his doorway.

A mixture of shame and relief seeped through Sharon, but her guilt at ignoring him wouldn't go away. She always gave generously to charities for the homeless, but that was sanitised giving where she did not have to deal directly with damaged, lonely people. She hated being accosted in the street, but it was her own fault. She shouldn't have stared at him.

She stopped by the cash machine and inserted her card. Her pin had vanished from her mind and she had to try twice before she got it right. The notes slid out smoothly and silently, free from any guilt. She put them in her purse.

+ +

The man took another drink. The doorway wasn't the first he'd slept in, there were worse places and he knew them all. The dog helped to keep him warm and warned him if anyone came near. It didn't have a name, he just thought of it as "the dog", but he always made sure it didn't go hungry, even if he did.

He wondered about the posh cow in her posh suit and posh shoes gawping at him like that. It was rude, that was, downright rude. He'd always been told it was rude to stare when he was a little boy, but people today had no manners. They just treated him like a piece of trash. Just because he lived on the streets.

Well, whose fault was that? He hadn't asked to be taken into care. Care, huh! He took more care of the dog than they had of him.

'Hard to place,' they'd said.

'Out of control.'

One small, frightened, lonely little boy. Always moving him from place to place, in and out of foster homes, worse than his own home where they'd said he was "at risk", changing schools all the time, picked on and bullied, called thick by the teachers, never there long enough to learn, never there long enough to make friends.

He'd run away from the children's home to look for his own family. When he couldn't find them, he'd survived by stealing and begging, until he'd been caught and sent back, put in a home for "difficult" children. Punishment. That was what being in care was all about. They'd punished him for everything. Sometimes he'd believed they were punishing him for being born.

Then, as soon as he'd turned eighteen, it was bye-bye and out the door. They didn't care he'd got no job and nowhere to live. Not their responsibility any more. And once he was an adult, the next time he'd got nicked for thieving, he'd been sent to prison. Funny though, it was better than the children's home - nicer food, fewer rules and he'd learnt how to read. Even the bullies hadn't been as spiteful.

For a moment he was tempted to do something bad, just for a warm bed and a hot shower. Maybe rob that snooty bitch? She didn't have a clue. She looked as though she'd got plenty of money. He bet she'd never gone hungry in her life. And he wouldn't really hurt her, just threaten to, if she didn't hand the cash over. But what about the dog? He couldn't leave it, that would be wrong. The dog needed him. It depended on him.

He took another swig from his bottle. It was empty. If that hoity-toity madam had given him a couple of quid, but no, she was too mean. And what was a few quid to the likes of her? Nothing, that's what. She could afford it. Enraged, he hurled the bottle away and heard it smash satisfyingly on the pavement, scattering shards of glass. The dog barked excitedly and he aimed a kick at it. It missed, but then he'd intended it to. He would never hurt the dog. Dogs weren't mean or spiteful or vicious, not like people.

+ +

Sharon heard the noise of the bottle shattering and suddenly felt afraid. Memories flooded her with overwhelming intensity, brought to the surface by the sound of breaking glass. Memories she'd rather forget, buried deep in her mind, memories she never let herself remember. Voices raised in anger, in hate, shouting, yelling, never quiet. Smashed plates, broken bottles, broken windows, slammed doors, always the noise. She put her hands over her ears in an attempt to shut it out. The thud of fists on flesh, the sharp crack of a slap across the face, a leather strap whistling through the air. And the muffled sobbing, the frightened whimpers, the silent tears. The sounds of her childhood. They all came back to her in a terrifying rush, engulfing her with fear and sorrow.

Her emotions hit her with a physical force, like a foul blow to the stomach, and she paused to catch her breath. But her worst memory was still lying in wait for her and there was no way to avoid it, however hard she tried to force it back down into oblivion. New Year's Day. The day she had abandoned her little brother.

It had been a day like any other. Christmas and New Year weren't special in her house. She and Billy had learned not to ask why. When the screaming and shouting started, it was the same. But when the beating began, it was different. She thought it would never stop and she curled up in a corner, arms wrapped round her body, like the way the tramp's dog wrapped his tail around himself against the cold. As the boots left their marks on her, she prayed that this wouldn't be the time she died. The bruises were still there in her soul, too deep ever to heal. When it was over, she knew there was no hope for her and so she ran away, leaving Billy behind, alone.

The guilt would stay with her forever. She had promised to go back for him as soon as she had a place to live, but it wasn't soon enough. They were gone. The neighbours knew nothing, or so they said, and Social Services refused to help. She worked hard and kept searching, hiring private detectives, but there was no trace of Billy. She made a success of her life. It hadn't been easy, but now she had everything, a good job, a car and a house of her own.

It was no consolation. All her energies and all her money were spent looking for Billy. She had no-one to go home to, no-one to love, no-one to care for. What did she know of families except violence and cruelty? How could she have children of her own when she couldn't even look after her little brother?

She could still hear Billy's voice crying, begging her not to leave.

'Take me with you, Sharon,' he had pleaded. 'Don't leave me.'

+ +

As his voice receded into the past, the tramp and his dog shuffled up behind her again.

'Spare some change for a cuppa tea, Missus?'

Sharon turned round and, as she looked at him through eyes blurred with tears, she realised why he seemed so familiar.

'Billy?' she said.

'Yes, Missus, that's me, Billy,' he agreed, ready to say anything for the chance of some money.

'It's me, Sharon.'

'Yes, course you are, Missus,' he mumbled.

Sharon's eyes cleared and she saw that he wasn't Billy. He was sixty if he was a day and Billy wasn't yet thirty. How stupid to allow her imagination to run away with her. He stood there, swaying and smelling of drink, while the dog waited patiently at his feet. She opened her bag and took out her purse. There was two hundred pounds in it, the money she'd taken out from the cash machine earlier, the money for the private detective.

'Here take it, it's all I've got.'

She stuffed the notes into his grubby hands. Then, before he could speak, she turned away and almost ran back to the safety of her car, guilt soothed for another day, but her resolve strengthened. She would never give up hope. She would find Billy and they would be a family again.

+ +

He watched her go and then he counted the money, showing the wad of notes to the dog. The thought of all those bottles of booze made him feel warm inside and he decided to treat himself to the good stuff for a change. He had enough money to last him for weeks, and weeks was all he had if the doctor was to be believed.

'You'll be dead before you're thirty,' the doctor had said. 'You've got the body of a man twice your age.'

At the corner shop, he bought a bottle of malt whisky and a bar of chocolate, and a pack of doggie treats. The assistant hadn't wanted to serve him, but Sharon's twenty pound notes had soon changed his mind.

Back in his doorway, he and the dog settled down for the night. He gave the dog his treats and then took a long drink, raising the bottle in a toast to his benefactor.

'Thanks, Sharon,' he said. 'You finally cared.'

Fran Neatherway

January 6

A Village Christmas

I still love Christmas. I meet many people who say, mournfully, 'I don't like Christmas any more.' I agree there is too much commercialism today, but you can ignore it; you do not have to buy expensive presents you cannot afford putting yourself in debt for the next six months.

I am a Christian, not a very good one, still in training, but for me it should be about the baby born in a manger to save us. It should be a celebration of that story.

My Christmas always used to start on a local farm where my husband and I went to join a team plucking and dressing a few hundred turkeys, to earn money for presents and to provide us with a beautiful fresh turkey for our Christmas dinner.

The next thing we had was a mulled wine and mince pie service organised by our daughter with funny items and secular items all mixed up with sketches and songs played out by the Rainbows, Brownies and Guides with much singing, laughter and enjoyment. Then a crib service on early Christmas Eve with lots and lots of children and their families, very noisy and exciting.

Back in the day, we would carol sing round the village using torches and standing under the lamp-posts collecting money for charity. The children loved to do the collecting.

My Christmas couldn't start without these things. From my mother came the lucky dip tradition; we each bought five presents for one pound. They were wrapped up and then, at a given time, every one picked one. We all unwrapped them and if you were lucky you could swap it for something more suitable. I got much more fun buying those than the proper gifts.

We would go to church early on Christmas morning and the turkey would start to cook. Everyone would enjoy breakfast.

So that is why I still enjoy my Christmases. I do feel sorry for people on their own at this time and I wish I could ban all the extreme greed adverts from the television.

Ruth Hughes

January 7

A Feltwell Christmas

'I think I convinced her. I couldn't bear it if they said we can't be together at school, Ray, could you? We get so little time outside it.'

'And none at all over the holidays.' If I was spiteful to remind Tina of her upcoming trip to see her father in the States, that was surely less hurtful than saying I would trade all our public time together for those frustratingly rare and brief occasions when it was the two of us with nobody else around. I'd been sulking ever since she told me she would be away for Christmas and the New Year, and not because she would be going to Disney World. That in all honesty I could not picture her as part of the Roden family festivities was not the point. The point was, she should be as desperate for me as I was for her.

In my memory we had always been at Grandad Will's on Christmas Day. Uncle Dan was an intermittent figure, never failing to leave me a decent present even if he was not always there to see me open it. Today we arrived almost simultaneously with him and his Katiuska, making her debut with the wider family.

'And they say he might be getting *paid* to shag her. Jammy bastard.' I would echo my cousin Tom in explaining the residency question of my potential eastern European auntie to Omie ('I'll give it three months', Uncle Mike had apparently said). While I had not given Dan's fiancée five minutes' thought, I was not expecting to see what might have been a superfox sixth-former, if they had been allowed to wear fur boots and jackets. Her hair was all blonde ringlets, cascading down over big hooped earrings. She was hardly out of Dan's car before she was hugging Dad and a tight-lipped Mum. 'And you must be Dan's handsome nephew Ray, isn't it?' Delightedly she squeezed my cheeks between her gloved hands.

'No, it's the other one. This is ugly Ray.' Dan was evidently pleased at the impact his girlfriend had made. She was rather more sedate in greeting Nan and Grandad, shaking his hand quite formally, having removed her mittens, before astonishing the older woman by taking her hand to her lips and kissing it. 'Such a pleasure to meet you at last, my Daniel's dear mother. I thank you so much for inviting me into your lovely home and family.' Nan looked at Grandad, gobsmacked.

'You coming, Father?' Dan asked, as he and Dad prepared to leave for the Oak, where they felt bound to support Ted's initiative of opening for the first time ever on a Christmas Day. 'Father?' he repeated as Grandad Will blanked him.

'Me? No, no fear. Shouldn't be allowed to open today.'

Getting into the car before anyone could tell me no, without thinking that my haste to get away with the other men might be a blow to Grandad, I heard Dan sounding off to Dad. 'Self-righteous old fart, like he's never been in a pub in his life. Some of the stories I heard about him from his brother Marcus, God rest him, they'd make your hair stand on end. I know things change when you're married, look at you, but at least you don't get smug about it and I know you still miss the old days sometimes.'

I knew that Dad was some years older than Mum. A few caustic comments from her over the years led me to think he had a somewhat adventurous life as a bachelor, insofar as I thought of him as anything but my boring old man. I saw another side to him that Christmas morning, not only insisting on a couple of his own choices from the seven he allowed me on the jukebox – the first time I ever heard Elvis' *American Trilogy* – but revealing unsuspected talent as a pool player. I would never have thought he could beat Uncle Dan, but neither of us could knock him off the table.

That hour or two in the pub was the best part of my Christmas. We didn't even get in trouble for it. Mum and Nan were often red-faced from cooking by the time we sat down to dinner, but today a little Hungarian cherry brandy might have added extra colour to their cheeks. 'This is delicious, love.' Mum beamed. 'What did you say it is Katie…? Parlinka, that's it. Try some, Pete, it's delicious.'

Later, some years later, I would realise that Dan and Katiuska had either been drinking that morning before arriving at Grandad's, or were perhaps still what Mum would call 'half cut' from the night before. Over the turkey Dan proudly explained how he had honoured Katiuska's traditions by allowing her to prepare a feast for him on Christmas Eve afternoon – something about fish soup and stuffed cabbage, didn't sound like much of a feast to me, but my fifteen-year-old cynicism told me he wasn't with Katiuska for her cooking.

The afternoon was generally spent in a state of torpor – verging on stupor today as far as Dad was concerned – by the men of the family. I was kicking a ball against Grandad's garage doors when the last of his children arrived with her family to inject fresh energy into the day. Aunt Rose, between Agnes and Dan in age, had married younger than Mum so that my two cousins were older than I. Tom, working with Uncle Mike on his farm, was at twenty already married with a child. Paul, the first in our family ever to go to university, was apparently staying with friends in Leeds over the holidays.

There was a further round of opening presents, and much cooing over Ellie Baba (I was inordinately proud that I had given Tom and Glenda's daughter the nickname adopted by the whole family). Dan pretended to put into her pudgy paws a small, untidily wrapped gift. 'Here sweetie pie, can you give this to Auntie Katie from Uncle Dan, please. There's a good girl.'

Of course it was a ring. The females formed a huddle around it, while Dan explained that he had given it to Katiuska the day before, no way he was risking a refusal in the middle of his family. She'd made him wrap it up again. 'Ray, do us a favour, will you? Go and fetch that tray of drinks out of the kitchen for us.'

I was happy to do so, a dozen proper shot glasses rather than the mishmash of wine and pop ones the women had been drinking from earlier. When Dad, still elated from the lunchtime session, proposed the 'panini' toast, fixing the bride-to-be's family name forever as Katie, she and Dan took their drinks in a strange way she must have showed him, kind of crooking their elbows round each other so they were almost bumping noses as they raised the glasses to their lips. Before I could be challenged, I grabbed an untaken glass, gulping down its contents and thinking for a second I had splashed acid on my tonsils.

Only Glenda, not much older than me, noticed my participation, without concern. 'Are we supposed to throw the glasses into the fire?' she asked doubtfully.

'No, that's the Greeks, darling,' Dan clarified. 'Besides, they're an extra little present for Mum.' He put his arm round Nan, who barely came up to his chest. 'Sorry I had to take 'em out of their box and you'll have to wash 'em up first.'

I didn't mention the tears I saw in Nan's eyes in my letter to Tina. I also soft-pedalled a bit on Katiuska's extreme hotness. I invited her to the wedding which would romantically – coincidentally, Dan tried to insist but no one was buying it – be on Valentine's Day. Until then Omie had generally been my plus one at family gatherings where Mum feared I would otherwise be isolated or bored, but he accepted his relegation with good grace. We were both learning girlfriend trumps even top mate.

David G Bailey

This is an edited extract from David's novel *Them Feltwell Boys*.

January 8

Jane's Terror

'Jane,' Brian uttered.

'Hang on,' Jane replied with desperation, her eyes glued to the TV set. 'I can't believe it. They've just gone into the house. There's definitely something wrong with that house.'

'I need to talk to you,' Brian said.

'Shh! It's finishing in a minute.'

'Please, Jane. It's urgent.'

'You'll have my full attention in four minutes.'

Jane covered her face with her hands, before promptly peeking through her fingers at the screen.

'Don't go in there!' she yelled, as if the characters could hear her.

'Jane! Please. Can't you press pause for just a second?' Brian pleaded.

'No! I've got to know what's going to happen. Just give me three minutes. Don't go in there!'

She heard Brian move around, as if he were looking for something.

'Touch that remote and we're getting a divorce,' she said, her eyes not moving from the two detectives who were creeping through darkened rooms.

'Jane, enough! Can you look at me? I need to speak to you.'

'Two minutes. You can wait two minutes, surely.' She threw her hands across her face again as the floorboards creaked below the protagonists. 'I think it's a ghost. Or a murderer. Or it could be a wild bear? I have to know.'

'Jane! I need you to look at me.'

'It is! It's a murderer. I knew it!'

'Jane, please!'

Jane knelt down right before the TV as the characters opened the final door at the end of the landing. They stepped in and their eyes grew wide with utter shock.

'What the hell are you doing here?' one of the characters said, before dramatic music brought on the credits.

'No!' Jane moaned. 'Don't make me wait until next week. Who is in that room? I think it's a ghost. I said that bloke who died in the first episode was going to feature again.'

Jane turned her head towards Brian to finally look at him.

She screamed so violently, people streets away could have heard her.

'What has happened to you?' she yelled, as she took in the horror before her.

Lindsay Woodward

January 9

The Abbey Hotel

It had gone half past ten when they arrived, tired, frustrated, hungry, desperate for bed.

They had ordered dinner, but 10.30 was long past serving time. There were no customers in the bar, only the barman wiping the tables with a dirty cloth. It took a great deal of persuasion and frayed tempers before he agreed to drag himself into the kitchen to warm up whatever was left in the fridge and crash it down on the table in front of them. It was not appetising, gristly meat, reconstituted dried potato mash, a spoonful of peas.

'Could we have the keys to our room, please?'

'We don't supply room keys.'

'No room keys? What about security?'

'No problem. No other guests.'

'I would like to speak to the manager.'

'The manager is not available. He has been called away on family business. He will not be back until tomorrow evening.'

'What about the other staff?'

'There are no other staff, and I shall be going home myself as soon as I have cleared the bar.'

So it was almost midnight when they struggled up the stone staircase, past a small, grimy bathroom, to reach their bedroom at the top of the tower.

First impressions were not good. A massive four-poster bed was hung with tattered curtains, and a thick layer of dust covered all surfaces. Not the sort of place where you would want to spend more than one night, or at all. Richard groped for the light switch. A dismal, flickering light bulb hung from the ceiling.

'It's horrible!' Fiona shuddered, not wanting to touch any surface.

'You could have helped me with the luggage,' said Richard as he struggled out of a shoulder bag.

'We should have travelled light,' said Fiona. 'That spiral staircase has killed me.'

She wiped a chair with a tissue and flopped down.

'But, Fiona, you can just imagine the monks going up and down there.'

'They must have been a lot thinner then. And fitter. It is so steep.'

Richard pressed his point. 'But it's unique, isn't it. How many towers of ruined abbeys have you ever slept in?'

Fiona shivered.

'None yet, thank goodness. Just look at the bed. It's the sort of bed Ebenezer Scrooge would have slept in. Where he had his nightmares.'

Richard peered into the gloom. 'I admit, it doesn't look much like the photographs on the website.'

Fiona went over to the bed.

'The curtains are falling apart. The sheets don't look too clean. Do you think they have been changed since the previous occupants slept in them?'

'It's only for two nights.' Richard just wanted to sleep.

'I don't like it.' Fiona's voice shook. 'I don't fancy sleeping in that bed. Everything is covered with dust. Let's go somewhere else.'

'There isn't anywhere for miles. And I don't want to have to drive again after all those hills and narrow lanes. And it is pitch dark. I don't think this place is that bad. Regard it as an adventure.'

'And did you see the bathroom on the way up? It's like something out of the ark. I don't like the idea of groping my way down that spiral staircase to go to the loo in the middle of the night.'

'What did you expect, all mod cons? It's an abbey, for goodness' sake. And look, there's a torch here.

Fiona did not give up easily.

'It's so dismal in here. I bet that's a forty watt bulb.'

'They probably have their own generator, stuck out here miles from anywhere.'

Fiona pulled her coat closer.

'I read the abbey guidebook from cover to cover before my dinner arrived. Do you think it is true about this tower being haunted?'

'Of course not.'

'It could be true about the abbot falling down the stairs, though. Do you think this was the abbot's bedroom?'

'For goodness' sake, Fiona, it's all invented. Old abbey, so let's have a ghost, then people will want to come and stay here. And won't mind how much it costs.'

'Well, I don't want to stay here. It's spooky.'

'Look, I'm exhausted. All that driving down country lanes. And you were supposed to be navigating.'

'I told you we were going the wrong way.'

'I thought it would be a short cut. How was I to know the road was going to become so narrow and muddy, then that flooded section by that stream. We nearly got bogged. And all those hills and blind corners. And no signposts.'

'Well, listen to me next time.' Fiona was used to this. 'But this is awful. I'm not surprised there are no other guests.'

'Better than nothing, though, isn't it,' said Richard, yawning, 'and, it's too late now. The barman was desperate to get away. He will have gone home by now. And the manager has been called away, so he said. And he won't be back tonight. We've got a whole abbey to ourselves. Think of that. And, anyway, I like it. You were keen, too, if I remember rightly. And I've always wanted to stay here, ever since they converted the abbot's lodging into a hotel. And the beer's good.

'That's all you care about, whether the beer's good or not.'

'Very important, beer is, Fiona. I bet the monks brewed their own beer here. Better than drinking water, you know. You couldn't drink the water in medieval times. All the bugs were killed in the brewing process. So they drank beer. It's good for you.'

'I know, I know, as you have said before, a hundred times. Any excuse.'

'Well, let's get ourselves sorted.'

Richard opened his suitcase and took out his pyjamas.

'I'm not unpacking anything,' said Fiona. 'I don't like the idea of putting any of my clothes down anywhere.'

'You can't sleep in your clothes.'

'And I'm not having a wash tonight. That bathroom, so called, is horrendous.'

'Think yourself lucky that there is a bathroom. I bet the monks had to go out to an outhouse somewhere.'

'Serves them right for drinking so much beer.'

Richard changed tone. 'Well, bed, then. Come on, Fiona.'

'It's so cold. It's suddenly gone cold.'

'It'll be warm in bed.'

'No, can't you feel it? It has suddenly gone cold. I'm freezing. There's a really cold spot here. I don't like it, Richard.'

'For goodness sake, get in and stop being so ridiculous.'

'I'm not getting undressed. It's horrible here. I'm scared, Richard, really scared. '

'Look, we'll go somewhere else tomorrow, if you like, but tonight I'm staying here. So, please yourself.'

'I can't bear it, Richard. I feel something awful is going to happen.'

'Look, I've had enough of this, Fiona. I've been driving all day. You've given me a headache with your stupid rubbish. I'm tired, right? It's nearly midnight and I want to get into this bed and go to sleep. Got it?'

'You don't understand, Richard. It's all right for you. You don't care where you sleep. You don't care what you eat. You don't care about anything. You don't care about me either. If you cared about me you wouldn't have brought me here in the first place. I wanted to go to that hotel on the coast, but you wanted to stay in this filthy, dirty, primitive pigsty. That's what this is.'

'You said you wanted to come here.'

'Only because I knew it was no use arguing. You always get what you want, Richard. You just don't care. I hate you.'

'Fiona, will you shut up. You are driving me insane. Nothing ever satisfies you, does it? I slog away day after day so we can have some spare cash for a few days away, and you just carry on and on and on. There's just no let up.'

'And you always want your own way, don't you, Richard? You never consider my feelings at all. You never think about what I might want. Like having a baby. You don't want me to have a baby, do you? You are so selfish. You don't consider my needs at all, my maternal instincts.'

'I'm not listening to this, Fiona. We've had this out before. I've told you my reasons. When we get home, I tell you, this is all going to end. I've had enough.'

'You just want to shut your eyes and escape, don't you, Richard, instead of facing up to your responsibilities. You need to grow up, stop playing games. I mean, wanting to stay in an old ruin, like this. You are like a little boy playing at knights and castles.

Richard was angry now.

'Right, we're going home tomorrow. Some holiday this has turned out to be. I thought it would be romantic, staying in a historic building, in the hills, miles from civilisation. But no, home tomorrow. And that's it.'

'Please, Richard, just have a look on your mobile. See if there's somewhere else we can stay. Not tonight, but tomorrow. Please, so we can get away first thing in the morning. We don't need to go straight home. We'll find a proper hotel somewhere, or a b & b in a pretty little village, if you like. Please, Richard. Then I promise I won't complain any more. I'll stay here tonight, make the best of it, but please check on your mobile first.'

'All right. Just for a bit of peace and quiet. But I tell you, this is the last time I'm going to book any holidays. I can't stand the stress.'

Richard rummaged for his mobile and tried to connect.

'There probably isn't any reception, anyway. Oh, that's amazing! It's come up straight away.'

'Look for accommodation around here.'

'Only this place is showing. Tripadvisor.'

'What does it say?'

'Wait a minute. They mention the beer. A moan about the curtains, general cleanliness. Somebody commenting on the poor quality of the bacon for breakfast. Here's one about...'

He stopped.

'About what? Richard, about what?'

'Nothing. Nothing really.'

'Let me see.' Fiona snatched the phone and read.

'We could not sleep all night. Our room in the tower was very cold. At about midnight, we heard a noise on the stairs, then a scream and a crash as if someone had fallen. I got out of bed but the light did not work, so I took the torch and went to look but there was no-one there. We were terrified.'

'Richard! It's like the guidebook said. Richard, I'm frightened.'

'It's all nonsense. Somebody having a joke. Perhaps one of the staff had upset them. Or the meal wasn't up to their expectations. You know the type. They have to wait half an hour to be served, so they give a bad report. You don't want to take any notice of that.'

'But they said the room was cold. It is cold, Richard. I'm frozen.'

'Look, Fiona. Don't believe everything you read. It's somebody having a joke.'

'Or they had drunk too much beer.' Richard laughed.

'Or they'd been watching horror films on telly.'

'Or they were writers getting ideas for a plot.'

They were both laughing now, forgetting their quarrel.

'Or they were youngsters trying to scare everybody.'

'Or they were dreaming.'

Richard turned back the covers.

'Come to bed.'

'Wait while I get undressed.'

'I'll see to that.'

'It is so cold.'

'I'll warm you.'

'Even my feet?'

'Especially your feet.'

'Ready?'

'Ready.'

Suddenly, Fiona stopped, listened

'Did you hear that?'

'No. What?

'That noise on the stairs. Listen. Richard, listen.'

'I can't hear anything.'

'Shh! There's somebody out there.'

'Fiona, you are imagining things.'

'No, Richard. I can hear someone.'

'Come to bed.'

'No, someone is on the stairs.'

'It will be the manager coming back.'

'The man in the bar said he wouldn't be back until tomorrow evening.'

'Well, he must have changed his mind.'

'No. It's what they wrote, those people, on Tripadvisor, about the abbot who fell down the stairs.

'I can't hear anything. Fiona, I'm dead tired.'

'Richard, please. It's coming true. Can't you hear him?'

The light flickered and they were in darkness.

'Damn. The generator has switched off. It must switch off at midnight.'

'Where's that torch? Richard, please, where's the torch?'

Richard got out of bed and groped in the dark for the torch. He switched it on.

'There won't be anyone there,' he grumbled. 'But to please you, I'll go and have a look.'

'No! Richard, don't go. There's something horrible out there. Stay here with me. Please, Richard!'

'Fiona, stop this! You are being hysterical. Come and see for yourself.'

'No! No! '

Richard opened the door and stepped onto the tiny landing.

'Look, there's nothing there. Damn! Now the torch has gone out. I can't see a thing.'

But Fiona heard his footsteps on the stone steps, then his frightened cry, and the sound of his body falling and tumbling down the stairs.

Wendy Goulstone

January 10

Gold

Frank stared out of the window. It was a chilly morning. Three of the care assistants were huddled in a group outside smoking fags and scrolling through their social media. This is what life had come to. He'd been in the home for seven years now. The weekly bin collections seemed to be coming round with increasing rapidity. Shepherd's pie for lunch again today. What was the bloody point of anything anymore?

For some unknown reason, there was a break in the clouds and a ray of sun flashed across the wall next to him and then was gone. Golden sun.

And he was transported. He was back there with her, in the midst of that first, beautiful exchange of truths, that whispered conversation, that acknowledgement of something amazing bursting through, something life-changing.

He was touching her arm again, gently, not with menace but with invited, comfortable tenderness that meant you are treasured and I will treasure you. He was running his fingers through her long hair, surprised by its softness, luxuriating in its flow and chaos. He knew, he knew. Then he was caressing her orange dress that he liked to think of as gold, its lilting almost tissue-like linen tenderness which matched her personality, so frail yet so wise, so independent yet so needy - and it was he, Frank, who was being given the privilege to be the one who would guide her and shelter her through life, and be there to see her laugh, prosper and fly into the person she was meant to be.

The golden dress had fallen away onto the floor and they were lovers. Oh and it was so perfect, so perfect. Everything, everything...

There was a knock on Frank's door.

"Laundry is back, Frank. Shall I put it away?" said slightly-friendly

Becca. Frank nodded. Becca opened the wardrobe and hung up Frank's jacket. Next to that flash of gold.

John Howes

January 11

'Panic' Isn't In The Geordie Dialect

Descending the fell was no challenge to my affliction, a fear of heights. We came down the second quickest way (not many survive the quickest). There was a wide slope with a rather worn-down scree – a whole fellside of loose small rocks. We scree-ran almost all the way down. No problem: dig heels well in, don't lean forward and just run down along with all the rocks you set rolling, hoping you'll keep pace with them. Not good for the boots, but oh so thrilling. That scree looks vertical in the photo I took of it later and, even though I know it's not, it makes me feel so good. Our guide was a last-minute replacement for his friend, the official one. He'd led us to the fell-top by taking us up a stream.

The second day the Geordie decided to scrap this cissie kind of thing and give us a real challenge: abseiling.

The hard part is the start. There's a safety rope tied around you and you have another which you move along down, feeding it out around yourself as you control your speed of descent. To start you lean out backwards from the top of a cliff. I went over fighting my instincts all the way. I created my own technique: staring at the rope-feeder who was soon to look down on me. 'Talk to me,' I begged. 'Talk to me. It helps.' The dozen of us all managed it.

Our reward was a taller cliff. We were allowed to – perhaps 'drop out' isn't the suitable phrase – to 'decline' and some did. All strangers to each other, there was no one to take tales back home. I used my special technique of abject begging plus starting off kneeling. I just couldn't lean out backwards standing up. At the top of a cliff.

Eventually all of us gathered at the top of the third and final cliff.

It was as big as the building where I worked, four tall storeys of it. Anything taller was limited by the length and weight of rope possible. And it had a huge cave mouth at the base where you'd be descending through fresh air, illogically somehow more threatening than alongside sheer rock. It boggled my mind.

+   +

I voted with my feet, which bore me to the base with an increased number of companions.

I stood at the bottom and looked at the few small figures up there. And I knew, I just knew, I had to go back up. Can't explain it. I had no choice, it seemed.

'God, your face, Chris, when you arrived back up,' I was told, thankfully later.

'I had to look away, I was laughing so much,' said the Geordie's helper, specially roped in, as it were, for the occasion. 'Your face was white. A picture.'

My special technique was intensified. It took some time for me to talk myself over. My hardened safety-rope-feeder had to look away again, I was told later. Once over, it became easier. You held the other rope out to the right to descend and brought it in to slow and brake. I developed a pleasing rhythm, which allayed my fear, somewhat.

And then the feeder rope suddenly stopped. A bulge of rock blocked my view upwards. 'Hang on, Chris,' I heard. Hang on! It was all I could do, motionless, about a third of the way down. What now? I thought, in some suspense. I couldn't even panic. Does panic, like hysteria, need an audience? I was alone. I could hardly frenziedly run around, so I did as instructed, I hung on. Like a spider at the end of its silk. I remembered I'd seen spiders like that who'd suddenly swiftly descend as their silk unexpectedly lengthened.

My fate was in the hands of strangers somewhere above whose voices I could just about hear. I repeated my mantra: Out to descend, in to brake. My rope occasionally vibrated and jiggled me about. Will they have to get help? Will they pull me up? How? I could be hanging around for ages. Out to descend – alone. It could get dark.

Out-to-descend, in-to-brake. Out-to-descend...

Or lower me down? It's a long way... Out-to- descend, in-to-br... a shout came down for me to continue.

+ +

They didn't shout out any explanation, but told me later. It hadn't been some evil Geordie sense of humour. They'd realised the safety rope was feeding out over a rock - was in danger of being frayed, I'm afraid.

I descended in rhythm. Passing the gap of the cave was thrilling - but nothing like my meeting with terra firma. Relief. Exhilaration. Pride. And this is where as a writer, I come up against my inadequacy at describing my feelings then. I cannot command the words.

If this were fiction, this where it would end, but this is memoir, and our Geordie had yet more thrills of abseiling to offer. Underground. In the dark.

Gathered outside the mineshaft, we put on head-lights. One by one we were going to descend some way and feel with our feet for the ledge – once found, keep close to the 'wall' - the ledge is narrow and there's a long drop from it – then unhook the rope and send it back up for the next. Any volunteers to be first?

Not me.

Profound is my admiration for the woman who did. How could she? To descend into the dark in hopes of feeling for a narrow ledge and then wait with no safety rope alone in the dark. Did she go on to rule empires? Or did she simply have no imagination? It raises all sorts of questions about bravery. I write. I have an imagination. I made sure I went second. The reality of being down there would be easier than waiting up there, in the light, the victim of my own imagination as I pondered my immediate future. We talked to each other as I descended. However brave my words, fear distorted my voice, deepening it. The tones of the men in the group were distorted, too, as they descended, despite their having less licence to reveal fear. Their minds had chosen the words; their voices couldn't deliver.

+ +

All down, we shuffled along, keeping close together. The torches just emphasised the immensity of the surrounding dark but soon shone on a much wider path, still, however, edged on the left with an abyss of unknown depth. High with relief, we spaced out and strode on, keeping close, I noticed, to the rock-face on our right.

My torch suddenly revealed a beautiful strange fungus growing up from the path ahead, a small white sausage-shape covered in glowing delicate filaments. I drew the others' attention to it in wonder and bending down for a closer look, found it was a discarded tampon.

I thought of its previous owner. When a girl's got to go…I hoped her companions had waited, at a suitably discreet distance, for her, surrounded by dark, the only illumination firmly fixed to her head. It meant, I realised, that others had used this route, and it was possibly a well-known one. It was a kind of retrospective comfort; the first comforting thought I'd had the whole week-end. It was long before Health and Safety, of course. Our Geordie confessed he had gone a tad beyond his friend's remit, a bit, perhaps. He'd wanted to make things interesting for us. 'Profoundly grateful to him' is the cliché I must give him. He made things interesting.

When I returned to work I found myself for a month looking up at that tall four-storey building, with dismissive smugness.

Chris Rowe

January 12

Ninety-One

Ninety-One was the number of our house in Coppice View Road where we went to live when I was six and my brother five. It was a council house, over the road were private houses and I do not think they were very pleased to get us opposite them.

We had a gas fire and a real bathroom with a real bath, no more tin bath in front of the fire! We were seven minutes from our primary school which was new and modern. We were also only ten minutes away from Sutton Park entrance too.

Sometimes we would walk across The Park to my nanna Kate's house, my mum's mum. She lived on Sutton Parade. When I got a little older I would be allowed to go and get shopping for her.

She liked middlecut back bacon on number six, and sugar and tea came in blue paper wraps. I have never tasted cheddar cheese as good as hers, served up with a crust of her big white loaf, nectar! When my grandmother wanted to say something private to our mum, we were ushered outside to play. Little pigs have big ears, she would say..

Sometimes we were left with Nanna to look after us. She would take us up to be with her, one on each side of her. She would tell us the story of the three little pigs, with so many extra bits to it until we fell asleep.

We were very happy at Ninety-One. We played with the neighbouring kids and our cousins came over and we all went in the park together with picnics. There was a stream where we could paddle, catch sticklebacks and crayfish and build dams.

I didn't leave there until I went off farming. Sometimes I still dream of being back at that house and not understanding that there is no one still there.

Ruth Hughes

January 13

Matilda And The Little Blue Dog

Matilda enjoyed following Little Blue Dog. Her toy doll feet were so quiet on the pavement of Funborough: a town of rainbow colours, crazy fun houses; one like a biscuit tin, one was a policeman's hat and they all seemed to be built with play dough. The streets were the same colour as on the town map! She loved his little adventures. Today, he did a double take at the butcher's shop which was decorated with purple sausages. Yummy.

Matilda made the mistake of looking down at her hands.

"That's impossible! They're plastic," said a voice she didn't recognise and didn't know where it came from.

Matilda focused on the antics of the Little Blue Dog as he tried to distract the butcher and get some other delicious multicoloured meats, every time getting closer to his target.

Everyone who walked past, every toy, giggled to see the butcher chase the dog and trip over the cat, and even Matilda smiled.

Suddenly the brilliant colours of the town faded to beige and then to darkness. Tilda took off her virtual reality goggles.

"Gemma, this is amazing! I feel so much better, after just hiding in there for a few hours!

"It was all built from your childhood stories you supplied," said Dr Gemma Fyne.

"Those were the tales my dad told to me when I was a toddler."

"That's the idea, a rest from reality, Tilda, When you lost your family I had to do something for my old friend. One day, we might be able to help others with their grief and pain," said Fyne.

Tilda spoke softly. "Has it been two years already? Grief makes everything pointless, even the calendar, Gemma."

"Come back for an afternoon session and you can play the butcher this time. I think that'll help."

The old friends hugged.

Chris Wright

January 14

The Fate Of Fifty-Two

It was singles night at the Satin nightclub. Ruby looked dazzling in her short sparkly dress and glittering make-up, and she was convinced that tonight she'd meet her dream man. She could feel it in her bones.

After she and her friends had paid their ten pound entry fee, they stepped forward to receive their pegs. Every woman and man picked a peg from the relevant bag. The aim was to find the person who had the same number peg as you, and then you were supposed to kiss.

In Ruby's head, this was incredibly romantic.

She picked her peg from the bag and studied the number. Fifty-two. That was a good number. Now all she had to do was find the sexy man who had the other same numbered peg and she would be on the road to love.

Most people just headed to the bar. Most people didn't seem to care. A few people casually asked others about their number. But Ruby was on a mission.

She asked dozens of men across the four rooms of the nightclub before she finally found her match.

He was indeed handsome. And there was a spice to his aftershave that warmed Ruby in every place that mattered.

'You're fifty-two?' he asked with a look of disappointment.

'Yes. I think you owe me a kiss.'

'I'm just here for a laugh,' he replied, shaking his head. Her gorgeous match looked around. 'Mate,' he called to a random passer-by. 'Are you here to hook up tonight?'

'Yes!' the man replied.

'Here. Have my peg. She's your match. Best of luck.'

Mr Gorgeous sauntered away, leaving Ruby left with the less attractive option. He was skinny, untidy and smelt vaguely of petrol.

He smiled enthusiastically. 'You want a drink?' he asked.

This could not be happening.

'There's been a mistake,' Ruby replied. 'I'm twenty-five not fifty-two.'

'You're kidding! This is fate! That was the number of my first peg.'

No, this really couldn't be happening.

Ruby begged for other women that night to swap their pegs with her. No one did. And the skinny man followed her around until she finally gave in at around midnight and headed home alone.

Her romantic dreams were dashed. But what would fate have in store for Ruby at the next singles night? She held on to her hope and she remained ever positive.

Lindsay Woodward

January 15

In The Mist

'Can we just stop for a minute? I'm puffed.'

'Not if we are to get to the top before the weather cuts in.'

There was an edge to Alan's voice, sharp, impatient. Sarah had climbed only a few of the lower summits, mere hills by comparison, and not in winter. Why did she persuade Kelly to let her join the party?

'It's cut in already. I can't see where I'm going.' Sarah wished she was at home, feet up on the sofa, the cat purring on her lap.

'It's not far, now, just don't lag behind. Another half hour or so and we'll be there.'

'Could we slow down a bit, Kelly? I can't keep up.'

'It's better to keep going, Sarah. Keeps your heart pumping the blood round.'

Why hadn't she been firm and told Sarah that she was not sufficiently experienced to tackle such a stiff climb? Now Kelly felt responsible, as if a rope was dragging her back.

'You can say that, Kelly. I bet this is a piece of cake for you.'

'And stop talking. Save your breath. Come on or we'll lose them.'

Alan had already faded into the mist. Kelly was a good climber, careful, steady, but Alan's long legs and sheer strength enabled him to cover more ground more quickly. He soon caught up with Dan.

'Where are the girls?' asked Dan.

'Kelly's fine, a great walker, tough as nails, but Sarah, she's lagging behind. She shouldn't have come.'

'You are supposed to be bringing up the rear.'

Dan felt the responsibility. They should have stayed together.

'Kelly's been up before a few times. She knows the way.'

'I can't see them. The mist has obscured the path, what path there is.'

'They'll be all right.' Alan sensed the criticism.

'I'm not so sure. Sarah has precious little experience.'

'She shouldn't have come. She's a handicap, but she was dead keen.'

'She's keen on you, Alan, not the mountains.'

'She's a bonny lass, but not my type, you know.'

'We all know your type, Alan, even if Sarah doesn't.'

+ +

'Kelly, please stop. I've got to stop. There's something in my boot, a pebble or something. It's rubbing my heel. It's really painful. Please stay with me. I want to get it out.'

'Can't it wait? We must be nearly there. We can't waste any time. It's getting darker already and the mist is closing in.'

'It really hurts. I can't go on like this.'

Kelly turned down her mit and looked at her watch.

'Be quick then, or we'll be in trouble. Dan has a schedule.'

'Dan's a slave driver.'

'He's a great climber.'

'He's not very sympathetic. I prefer Alan.'

'That's obvious.'

'Is it?'

'You are wasting your time.'

'Has he got a girlfriend?'

'Girlfriend? No, not a girlfriend. Now stop talking and hurry up.'

+ +

Another ten minutes and they were on the summit ridge, jagged, crags dropping either side. A few inches of snow filled the gaps between rocks. Alan picked his way.

'Watch your step here, Alan. It's icy. Can you see the girls?'

'No sign.'

'We should go back.'

'We could make a quick dash then meet them on our way back.' Alan wasn't going to let a woman ruin his day. 'She's a nuisance, that girl. Held us all up, and now we're short of time.'

'She's Kelly's friend. I thought she'd be all right.'

'She's a novice, a handicap. Dan, you should have put her off. And you shouldn't have gone crashing on ahead. We shouldn't have split up.'

'Are you criticising my leadership?' Dan knew Alan was right.

'I'm just saying, you shouldn't have left them to fend for themselves.'

'And what about you, Alan? How come you are up here with me?'

'Passing the buck, are you? Of course, that's you all along, isn't it, Dan?'

'Look, if you are that worried, why don't you trot off down and play nursemaid to the little girls?'

'I can't leave you on your own. It isn't done.'

'Look, mate, I know every inch of this mountain. I don't need you to hold my hand. Go on, off you go. Go and play with your little friends. Go on, clear off and let me get on.'

'Right, if you feel like that, I'm going back. Take care, there's ice.'

'Go. I don't need you to nursemaid me. Go on. Clear off.'

So Alan, furious now, turned back along the ridge.

 + +

'Is your foot all right, Sarah? How does it feel?'

Sarah inspected the damage. 'There's a blister. Kelly, have you got a plaster?'

'Wait a minute while I find one.'

Kelly sighed, struggled her arms out of her rucksack and rummaged for her first aid pack.

Sarah thought of hot chocolate, a warm dressing gown, bed.

'Sorry to be a nuisance.'

'You can say that again.'

'I shouldn't have come.'

 + +

Kelly had told her it was a tough mountain, but it wasn't just the climb. The weather had deteriorated while they waited there. The cold bit their cheeks and Sarah's glasses had steamed up as the mist closed in.

'Here. Stick this on your heel.'

'I can't get at it, all these clothes, it's a struggle.'

'Give me your foot. I'll do it.'

'Thanks, Kelly. I'm sorry.'

+ +

'Oh good, here you are.' Alan's voice made them jump. 'I think you should go down.'

'Alan, thank you. I'm done in, to be honest.' Sarah felt her cheeks blush.

'So, I'll see you and Kelly down to below the mist.'

'Where's Dan?' Kelly's turn to be anxious.

'He's gone on.'

'On his own? That wasn't wise.'

'He insisted. He knows the way.'

'But the weather. You know the code, Alan. Don't climb alone.'

'He's stubborn. He'll do what he wants to do, irrespective of anyone else.'

'I've spoilt everyone's day.'

'Sarah, you have more sense than the lot of us put together. We should all have turned back.' Alan was warming to her. Pity she was a girl.

'You can't just leave him.'

'His choice.'

'I'm going up.'

'Kelly, you'll kill yourself There's ice and snow up there. Black ice, treacherous, slippery as hell.'

'I'm going up. I'll wait for him at the start of the summit ridge. Give him a shout. Get him to come back.'

'He won't come.'

'Wait for me, here, in the shelter of the rock. Huddle together to keep warm. If we are not back in an hour, go down and get help.'

+ +

Alan looked at his watch again. Forty-nine minutes. There was still time. Sarah was huddled by his side, hunched over, shivering, her feet and fingers numb

'Huddle up, Alan, keep me warm. Put your arm round me, please.'

'I should go and look for them.'

'Kelly said wait for an hour.'

'They should be down by now. I'm going up. I'll leave my pack. Put it on top of your feet. And here, take my mitts. And my scarf. Don't go away.'

'Alan, I'm scared. Please don't go.'

'I have to. Wait here.'

+ +

This is the nine o'clock news: Two bodies have been recovered from below a cliff in the Scottish Highlands. A third person reported to be with the party is still missing and weather conditions have hampered search and rescue teams. A woman is in hospital recovering from exposure. Ice, snow and freezing mist continue to be forecast for the Grampians and surrounding areas of Scotland.

Wendy Goulstone

January 16

The Last Second

Fred Greenhalgh took a step back, and regarded his work. He stood, with his detail brush in his mouth, and his wide brush dripping dark paint onto the old sheet spread out on the floor.

"Second !" he yelled, "How does it look from there ?"

'Second' was near the back of the church hall, marvelling at Fred's ability to make a piece of flat canvas look like a castle wall, and at his ability to talk clearly with the paintbrush clamped securely between his teeth. "It's just right," and she joined him on the stage.

"Just the lighting to do, and then we can bugger off home." Fred grinned at his young apprentice, pleased to note she wasn't taken aback by his colourful language. She was just a young thing, no longer a little girl, not quite a woman. Fourteen, or thereabouts, he reckoned. But she was the best sidekick he'd had in the last five years as chief scenery painter, electrician, props man and general miracle worker for this group of amateur 'theatricals'. She followed instructions, wasn't afraid to ask when she didn't quite understand, and she had a wicked sense of humour.

He watched her wiring a plug onto a longer cable, setting up the labels on the faders, arranging all the leads so that there were no tangles, and testing each light before Fred climbed up to hang them on their respective stands. He liked the little smile that touched her mouth when she finished each job. She didn't expect praise, or even thanks, but when he said, 'Job done. Grand,' she lit up like the moon.

It was late when they set off together to go home. The snow crunched under their feet, their breath hung in the air, freezing their words. When they reached the deserted chip-shop their paths took different directions, but they paused for a few last words.

"Goodnight then, see you tomorrow."

"Goodnight Fred," and she smiled and walked off down the road, humming *In the bleak mid-winter*, disappearing into the dark. Fred turned for home. And he never saw her again.

EE Blythe

January 17

Calm Attic Spaghetti

As I was measuring spaghetti, Adam ran into the kitchen.

'Hey, Tanya! Look what I found in the attic!' he said, holding out a dusty wooden box, and wiping his sleeve across it. Brass inlay glinted against the dull wood.

'Pretty,' I said, touching the ornate scrolls engraved on the hasps. 'Where was it?'

'By the chimney breast. I put the Christmas decs there and saw something covered in masses of cobwebs. Honestly, Tanya, I swear the spiders there are big enough to take on a mouse and win.'

I shivered. 'Ugh! Rather you up there than me.'

He slowly opened the lid. 'And look what's inside.'

Several glass jars lay on their sides, showing labels with neat faded lettering. Adam lifted one and read the label.

'Zesty spice and herb mix. Adds life to dull stews and sauces.'

He opened it. Suddenly a strange, savoury smell filled the air.

'Oh my God,' I exclaimed. 'Oh, wow! That smells amazing!'

We both drew in deep breaths.

'Like really expensive red wine, or like... like those dark mushrooms wrapped in bacon,' Adam murmured.

'I can smell basil, lemon, pepper, something else too. Coriander? Something, oh, it makes me think of roast lamb with garlic and wood fires and dark chocolate and – and just pure deliciousness.'

Adam turned and prodded the bolognese sauce with a wooden spoon.

'Shall we put some in here?'

I looked at the contents. Pale, watery, with hopeless fragments of onion drifting through the grey-tinged cheap mince and supermarket basic tinned tomatoes.

'Hmm. I dunno. We don't know what's in it,' I said.

'It'll be fine,' said Adam enthusiastically. 'Remember that bottle of blackberry whiskey we found at the back of the cupboard?'

I hesitated. The woman we'd bought the house from had been very odd: staring eyes, long plaits of jet black hair, dirndl skirt draped with fringed shawls; wearing bracelets and necklaces dripping with charms and seashells and pieces of coloured glass. But the whiskey had been exquisite, extra-ordinary. We'd drunk the whole lot to toast our new house and – to our relief – woken up the next morning feeling fantastic and with no trace of hangovers.

'OK,' I said.

Adam poured half the contents into the sauce.

'Steady on!' I started to say, but stopped as the delicious smell strengthened and the pallid bolognese thickened and deepened to a rich, warm sauce the colour of mahogany or roasted beef.

+ +

When the spaghetti was cooked, we decided to eat properly, at the table rather than watching some rubbish telly. Adam got a jazz mix playing on the Bluetooth speakers and we lit a candle. The sauce glistened on the pale yellow strands of pasta. I paused to savour the scent then wound the spaghetti through the sauce and onto my fork.

The taste filled my mouth, my whole senses, with flavours of beef, tomato, basic, garlic, umami, red wine and some deep, subtle tang I couldn't identify. I ate slowly, savouring every moment. Adam was rapt, staring at his bowl, swallowing then thoughtfully twisting his fork in the pasta.

'That's odd,' he said.

'What?'

'Did you see that?'

He pushed his fork through the sauce-coated spaghetti.

'It moved...' he said.

'What!' I said, and leapt up.

'Yeah – it's moving!' he said, leaping up too.

We stared at our bowls. He was right. The strands of pasta were stirring. There seemed to be more sauce and more spaghetti in the bowls. It was moving and growing. The bowls were fuller. As we watched, the sauce-covered pasta overflowed onto the table.

'Oh, shitake mushrooms...' I whispered and clutched Adam's hand. 'What's happening?'

'I don't know!'

The strands were thickening and writhing over the table. One slithered towards me and reached out, waving like a tentacle. We shrank back against the wall.

'It's like *The Little Shop of Horrors*!' I gasped.

'Don't be silly! It's bloody amazing!'

A long strand wavered and stretched towards him.

'Don't touch it!' I yelled, but it was too late. Adam reached out and took it.

Suddenly, more strands, now as thick as my fingers, rose up from the bolognese covered table. They moved and twirled and, to my astonishment, slid to the floor then upwards. They twisted into two strange shapes.

'They're alive... like... ' I whispered.

'Yeah - like people!' Adam said. He was right. The spaghetti had formed two flowing, intertwined figures with arms, legs and waving pasta hair, all glistening and dripping with the red, unctuous sauce.

Both figures bowed to us. The shorter one reached out a tentacle... arm... hand? towards Adam. He took it.

'They're friendly,' he said, smiling.

The figure started to gently sway to and fro in time to the music.

'It wants to dance!'

Adam took its hand, put his arm around the intertwined strands of its body and waltzed round the table as the sauce dripped and spread across the floor.

I laughed hysterically. Then the other figure took my hand and I too was swept into a mad dance.

'Waltzing spaghetti, waltzing spaghetti,' sang Adam as they swayed and twirled out into the hall. We followed, dancing too, while the scent of basil and tomatoes and mushrooms and that strange dark pungency filled the air.

More pasta figures appeared in the doorway to the dining room, and a tide of sauce crept around our feet as we pranced up and down the hall. My foot slipped but my strange partner held me tight. I looked at the slippery interwoven strands forming a pale, featureless mass instead of a face and suddenly I shivered.

'I don't like this, Adam,' I said, as we danced past.

'Think I've had enough too,' he gasped.

Feeling oddly weird, I said to my spaghetti partner, 'Thank you, but I'd like to stop now... please?'

It shook its head.

I let go of its hand and pushed it away with all my strength. Adam did the same. We'd reached the stairs and both, instinctively, stepped upwards to escape the pool of sauce on the floor.

The strange figures, now dozens of them, swayed towards us.

'Run!' I yelled.

We dashed up the stairs. The ladder was still there. We scrambled up it into the attic, pushed it away and dragged the hatch shut. Fortunately – typical Adam! – he'd left the light on.

Something pushed against the hatch. A pale thread snaked through the gap by the side of the hatch. I screamed as we scrabbled over the chipboard towards the chimney breast.

The hatch was pushed open. Several dreadful blank heads, dripping red sauce, rose through the hole and stared at us. I screamed again and clutched Adam's arm.

'Keep calm!' Adam yelled at me. 'I'm sure it will be fine!'

'Fine? Calm?' I yelled back. 'When we're about to be swallowed up by mad living spaghetti?'

'They're friendly, I'm sure...' Adam said.

Hysterical laughter shook me.

'Friendly? I don't bloody think so. They look furious. Probably mad 'cos we didn't put parmesan on that bloody sauce!'

Adam gasped. 'Say that again!'

'What? Bloody sauce?'

'No! Say it all again – all that last bit!'

'Probably mad 'cos we didn't put parmesan on that bloody sauce?'

'Parmesan...' Adam muttered. 'Yeah... look! Parmesan!'

The pasta figures seemed to hesitate.

'Parmesan!' Adam shouted. 'You lot just watch it! I've got a grater in the kitchen and I'm not afraid to use it!'

They wavered.

'Cheddar! Parmigiano!' he yelled. 'I'm warning you!'

They shrank visibly.

'Cheese! Grated cheese! Come on, Tanya, join in!'

'Parmesan. Cheddar. Red Leicester! Brie!' My voice grew louder. The weird figures were definitely getting smaller.

'Don't you remember?' Adam exclaimed. 'That Italian waitress saying you should never put cheese on a good bolognese sauce? That it killed the flavour?'

'Yes!' I said, nodding and shouting. 'Camembert! Wensleydale!'

'Goat's cheese! Blue Shropshire!'

They fell back through the hatch. Staring through the hole, yelling 'Mozzarella! Cheshire cheese!' we saw them cower and scamper down the ladder. We followed. With each shout, they quivered and diminished. As we reached the dining room, the sauce and spaghetti had reduced to a trembling heap on the table.

'Stilton!' Adam yelled. 'Rochefort!'

'Stinking Bishop!' I shouted triumphantly and with a faint gasp the heap vanished.

Calm silence filled the room. Even the strange scent had gone.

Adam and I looked at the empty bowls.

'That was weird,' he said.

'Yes,' I said. 'Very. But I'm still hungry. Um... how about fish and chips?'

Cathy Hemsley

A note on the title: Our writing group was set a challenge: to use the 'Take three nouns writing prompt' website to get three nouns, then write a story based on them. I was given 'calm attic spaghetti'.

January 18

Alter Ego

Recently on my way to book club I was cutting across that wide piece of corner paving by the exit of John Barford car park in Rugby when a woman came walking towards me. We had time to assess each other: about my age, dressed smart casual. It somehow registered that she looked my sort of person, someone I would readily have talked to in a group of strangers: interesting. She smiled as she drew level, stopped, proclaiming with delight, 'I've spoken to you before, in the car park of Walsgrave Hospital.' I was late for my meeting and knew I'd never been to the Walsgrave. Didn't even know where it was. Somewhere in Coventry, I thought, near the end of the Foleshill Road.

'Sorry, I'm late for a meeting,' was my uncivil response as I scurried past, almost immediately regretting not stopping.

Later in the book discussion, somewhat peeved, I regretted that I'd been in such a hurry to reject someone who wanted my full attention. Even later, by some weeks, I recollected that I had been to the Walsgrave, some decades earlier, admittedly. I was taken to the staff squash courts by one of the hospital's secretarial staff. She'd sign me in as a guest, we'd play our squash and socialise in the staff bar afterwards. I can't recall her name or how we became acquainted, but it was probably through squash. We were more or less equally matched; definitely not club standard but competent enough for an enjoyable game. Don't know why we stopped going. I suspect we'd started going because we got free access to the court. I can't remember her name, if I drove there or got a lift with her. The socialising in the bar, mingling with medics was a glamorous thrill. In those days a Mills and Boon Star Hero was a doctor. One thing I remember, clearly: at the bar afterwards, someone greeted me with surprised pleasure.

'Hello! Didn't realise you were back. How did you get on? What was it like working in Canada? Better than here, I bet. Wish I'd done it. Anyway, nice to see you're back.'

'Er,' my reply was swept away as people bustled by and the conversation moved on. I wondered what my job had been. I hoped I'd enjoyed it and got some skiing in.

So, be careful if you're greeted as an acquaintance. You never know what your alter ego may have been up to.

Chris Rowe

January 19

Winter

Surrounded by gentle hills that swept down through wooded slopes to the valley of the river Tweed, our tied cottage nestled on the side of what was known locally as the Roman mountain, with earthworks on the top that was allegedly occupied for a time by a small unit of Roman soldiers, who had the misfortune to be sent north of Hadrian's Wall to keep an eye of the truculent Caledonians.

It was still silent and pitch dark outside and the temperature was well below zero. Anyone who believes the saying 'It's too cold to snow' should visit Scotland in the winter. Jack Frost had painted breathtakingly beautiful pictures on the curtainless bedroom window, now illuminated by a small single wick paraffin lamp whose flickering light shifted and moved the sparkling artwork like some magical kaleidoscope as the glittering crystals reflected the flame. My Mother was already up in the wee small hours to see dad off to work milking the herd of thirty-odd cows on the farm.

We had no electricity in our house but downstairs was brilliantly illuminated by a paraffin lamp called a Tilley. The farm had its own generator to power the primitive milking machines and supply lights to the chickens so they would not stop laying twenty-four hours a day.

Downstairs I could hear Dad's pride and joy, the accumulator battery-powered radio giving the shipping forecast: 'Fair Isle, Viking, Forties, Northeast veering Northwest, three or four, occasionally six later, Thundery showers, Moderate or good, occasionally poor.' All this sounded completely contradictory and confusing to me but for some reason beyond my reasoning my father reckoned he could make sense of the forecast's utterances to guide him into what to expect from the local weather on the hills, that could for the inexperienced be a matter of life or death.

We lived many miles from the nearest town and schools so we had to get up at truly silly o'clock, dress, have breakfast and venture out before dawn in the depths of winter to the bus stop a mile away down the farm lane, many times in driving snow and bitter winds that froze one side of enormous snow drifts, while leaving the leeward side still soft, ready for foolhardy children to venture off the road that had been temporarily cleared by our farm tractor with a plough attached to make way for the milk wagon to pick up the day's milk churns. I soon learned the unpredictable nature of the drifts after my older brother had to dig me out a couple of times when I was that foolish child who thought he could walk on snow. By the time we reached the road end, the cardboard from the cornflake box I had inserted in my jumble sale shoes to cover a hole had long since disintegrated to a mush with my socks and feet soaked and freezing.

There was hardly ever a time, even in the worst conditions when the bus didn't run to get us to school, though there were times when we no sooner got there we had to set off home again in case we couldn't if the weather worsened. Looking back now, I still wonder that even in the harshest conditions life went on almost normally, buses and trains ran, schools and shops opened and most importantly for us on the farm the milk churns were collected for bottling at the dairy somewhere miles away.

The weekends were sheer bliss when we could stay in bed and not get up till the sun rose. One by one the six of us children, four boys and two girls, would make our way down the stairs to the heady smell of methylated spirits and paraffin used to fire up the Tilley lamp that lit up the room brighter than any incandescent electric lamp, but also provided an astounding amount of warmth complementing the heat from the fire. After breakfast, it was Wellingtons on and out to play, making dens in the snow piled up against the stone dykes or taking a packed dinner to my dad in the fields, digging out sheep after the final cow had been milked.

If the weekends were good, winter holidays were beyond fabulous with Lady Balfour in Stobo Castle providing a party every year in the village hall for all the local children in the village and farms, complete with lots of scrumptious cakes and lemonade and even better, Santa and toys for everyone, usually guns for the boys and dolls for the girls.

+ +

That was now more decades ago than I care to admit to, in an age just after World War Two when rationing prevailed with a shortage of many things. To see an aeroplane was something wonderful to behold, before ordinary country people had electricity or even decent plumbing in their houses and well before such things as telephones or TVs or so many things we now take for granted, but those magical winters still play in my minds eye when I want to drift off to a happy place.

We might have had holes in our shoes and cuts on our knees but we had riches beyond anything that money can buy, and we genuinely felt superior to those well-off town children who looked down on us just because we didn't have much in the way of perceived wealth. We never considered that life was hard, as it no doubt was for our parents; it just was what it was, with no holidays away, only second hand clothes and shoes, or anything else considered as a luxury in today's world, but by heaven contented and in our element as us kids were, I wouldn't want to go back to the early fifties now.

Patrick Garrett

January 20

La Belle Epoque

Jen and Ken had lived together for more than twenty years, though saying they lived 'together' was stretching it a bit. Jen was the music-lover and spent much of her time in her woman-cave at the back of the house; the vinyl carefully indexed not alphabetically but by the release date within the specific genre of music. She loved to while away the time exploring the intricacies of Joni Mitchell's *Hissing of Summer Lawns*. What was that song really about, Joni? You left it to us to decide, didn't you?

Meanwhile, Ken was in the kitchen with his cookery books. He loved the free rein of the food cupboards, space to create and experiment, room to be artistic with food that satisfied the eyes as well as the palate. When supper was ready, Ken would ring a little bell and meet Jen at the dining table like a guest at a dinner party. They would talk about their days as if they were strangers meeting for the first time and then depart, politely, for their respective parts of the house to pursue things they enjoyed. Was this what marriage had come to? Living together but apart? Or living apart but together?

It hadn't always been so. Remember that night at *La Belle Epoque*, the accordion player, the candlelight, the scent of Gitanes cigarettes, the sheer expectancy that something significant was going to happen - and it did, and they both knew it would be forever except nothing lasts forever and people change.

Ken tidied his cookery books and poured the last dregs of wine into his lonely glass. He wiped down the surfaces and switched on the dishwasher. Just as he liked, order had been restored to his domain. But now what? It was only a quarter to ten.

From the other side of the house, the strains of a record started filtering through to him. Piaf. *La Vie en Rose*. When was the last time he had heard that? Not for a lifetime, surely? And then it came to him. The singer at *La Belle Epoque* all those years ago. Bursting suddenly through the doors with her accordion in tow. She had been the soundtrack to Ken and Jen's big romantic moment. Everything made sense again. Their love had been sleeping but never absent.

He gulped down the last of his wine and turned towards the other end of the house and Jen's domain. He set off with purpose in his stride.

And hope.

John Howes

January 21

Trying To Make It

The wind whipped across the moor, churning the muddy pools lying in the bog. The light was already fading. This was not a night to be lost. He pulled his hood over his ears, slid down the zip of his anorak and took out the map. He battled to hold it as the wind tugged and tore, and he damned the loss of his compass. He estimated that he still had a mile to go, twenty minutes in good conditions, inestimable in this situation. He folded the map, shoved it into a pocket and staggered on, hoping he was not walking in circles. Would he be in time? He picked up speed, splashing through pools, his boots sinking and squelching, twice as heavy. Several times he fell. Now he didn't care if he made it to safety or if he lay down and died.

No, I can't kill him off, thought Janet, *I'm writing a novel, not flash fiction. I can't kill off my hero on the first page. I'd better start again.*

There was still a glimmer of sun as he set out across the moor, the dew sparkling on the moss. There was a little warmth in the light breeze, though the forecast was a heavy frost that night, the first of winter. There had been no rain for weeks, and the bog had dried up, so he was able to walk at a quick pace. No need to consult the map. He had been up here many times and could find his way in the dark. Just another mile to go. Twenty minutes and he would be there.

Oh dear, thought Janet. *Where's the challenge? Where's the conflict? I can't just let him arrive at the cottage, take off his boots, sit by the fire and eat the soup thrust into his hand by his loving mother/wife/ lover.*

He decided that the quickest way was to take the field path along the valley. He set out at a good pace, singing a folk song as he happily jogged along. He would soon be there, a little more than twenty minutes as this way was farther than the route across the moor. Mary would have hot soup waiting for him, and he would soon be sitting by the fire with her, telling her about the day's adventures. He stopped. In the distance he could hear the sound of roaring water. There had been a great deal of rain lately, and when he reached the river it was raging wildly. Where was the bridge? A few broken pieces of timber clung to a post as the water swirled by. What was he to do? The next bridge was in the village ten miles away. Could he wade across? Would he be swept away, or would he be able to swim to safety?

Oh sod it, thought Janet. *I'll write a poem tomorrow.*

She went into the kitchen, made a mug of cocoa, switched on the television, and put her feet up on the sofa.

Or maybe not.

Wendy Goulstone

January 22

Cliff Hanger

It might have been a beautiful day, but as we stepped through the forest of Cannock Chase, it all seemed terribly dark to me.

'You look scared,' my friend said, with her trademark nasty undertone. She was a master of belittling me behind a mask of true friendship.

But I was too young to know it. I was fourteen and afraid to break away from the norm. And the norm on that day was that falling off a cliff was fun. Or abseiling, as the others were calling it.

'I can't wait,' I replied. I was good at masking my own feelings.

My so-called friend was pumped with excitement. Maybe too much? I look back now and consider that maybe she was afraid too. But being human was a weakness. Unless it suited her, of course.

The demonstration was horrifying. They said you needed to lie flat as you made your way down the cliff. You needed to be horizontal. It wasn't like that in the movies.

I artfully steered my way to the back of the queue. If someone else fell to their death before me, surely I wouldn't be allowed my turn.

But my turn soon came around, and the girls who had already braved it were all smiling and happy.

I listened to every instruction as if my life depended on it. Well, it did. Shaking, sweating and wishing to be anywhere else in the world, I edged down the cliff. I couldn't afford to hesitate, for the mocking would be worse.

'You're not horizontal enough,' my friend shouted. I was quite sure my head was now below my feet. How could I not be horizontal enough? After what seemed like years of dangling down a cliff with nothing but a piece of rope to support me, I reached the bottom.

'Did you enjoy that?' my friend asked, ignoring my trembling frame.

'I'm glad I did it,' I lied, tactfully. 'But I don't know if I'd do it again. I found it really hard.'

'It's because you weren't horizontal enough.' She moved on to criticise me some more. I'd become used to it.

As we all headed back to the minibus (my favourite part of the whole day!), I said to myself over and over, I hope I never have to do anything like that again.

And believe me, I never have.

Lindsay Woodward

January 23

Teapot

It was an ordinary Saturday night in January. It wasn't dark and gloomy and mysterious. There was no full moon casting its eerie light over strangely shaped tree branches that tap-tap-tapped on window panes, no wind whistling eerily through the trees, no dramatic thunder and lightning, not even any romantic snowflakes gently falling and carpeting everywhere with a thick, white blanket that muffled the footsteps of passing strangers. It was cold and overcast and a little bit damp.

In the quiet, cosy warmth of her kitchen, Donna was making tea. It was her favourite room, practical yet cheerful, with stripped pine cupboards and cottage garden wallpaper. She hadn't bothered to close the flower patterned curtains and the rectangle of black nothingness above the sink drew her gaze as she filled the kettle. She plugged it in and switched it on, but something flickered on the edge of her vision. For a moment she thought she saw a teapot hovering in the darkness outside and she shook her head, telling herself not to be so silly.

The kettle clicked itself off, the sharp noise splintering the silence. Donna warmed the teapot, the sunshine yellow one, the first thing for their house that she and Dave had bought. To her, the bright colour had symbolised their happiness as they set up their new home together and she smiled at the memories, remembering how happy they had been, how much in love. She put the teabags in the pot and poured the boiling water over them, thinking there, that's killed the little buggers. The uncharacteristic thought surprised her and she laughed, stirring the tea more fiercely than usual.

From the corner of her eye she glimpsed a movement and turned towards the window, but all she could see was herself, mirrored in the darkness, a pale-faced figure holding a yellow teapot. But the figure streamed and elongated until there were dozens lined up behind the original, a caterpillar of special effects for a cheap science fiction movie. Donna rubbed her eyes and the strobe effect disappeared, leaving only one of herself. Oh dear, she thought, maybe I need glasses.

She took the tea things into the living room, where the television was on, the sound blaring, demanding attention. Dave was lying on the settee, TV remote control in one hand, bag of crisps in the other. He wasn't watching the programme; he was checking the football scores on his phone. Donna had seen him do this so many times before and it had never bothered her, but tonight she found it intensely irritating. He'd already seen the classified results at five o'clock. Surely they hadn't changed?

As Donna looked at the television, the lists of teams and points suddenly changed into rainbows of dancing teapots, waving their spouts as they undulated across the screen, getting smaller and smaller as more rows appeared. They changed direction, forming a Busby Berkeley kaleidoscope of chorus teapots. She put the tray down hard on the coffee table and the mugs rattled.

'Oh Dave, look at that,' she gasped, enthralled by the sight.

But Dave seemed unaware of the images. The teapots vanished, to be replaced by the weather forecast. He was only interested in the television gearing itself up for the highlight of his week - *Match of the Day*. Donna gazed at the screen in bewilderment. The little symbols on the weather map, sunshine, clouds, rain, had all been replaced by teapots. Even England looked teapot shaped, Cornwall the spout, East Anglia the handle.

Donna blinked her eyes hard and then looked at Dave, sprawled out in his dressing gown, revealing white hairy legs and flabby stomach. He'd been lying there most of the day, not bothering to get dressed. Donna didn't expect him to put on his suit, but he hadn't even showered. She made an effort. She went to the gym three times a week and the hairdresser every six weeks. Dave never noticed. She hadn't thought it would be like this; she and Dave would be different and keep their romance alight. *Match of the Day* passed by ignored and unwanted when they were first married, their bodies ablaze with love and passion. Now the flames barely licked her toes. When did it change? Why hadn't she noticed?

Dave was stuffing the crisps into his mouth, crumbs falling onto his chest. He brushed them onto the floor. He hadn't looked away from the television, which, Donna noticed, seemed to be developing a spout, lid and handle. His attention was focused on the screen, where a bearded teapot was talking about tonight's big match.

'That the tea? Thanks, babe.'

She hated being called that, always had done, even before they were married. It made her feel like a bimbo on one of those reality shows.

'Do you want arsenic with that?' she asked.

'Yeah, OK, love.'

I wish, she thought. Would he notice? Would I care?

Without looking, Dave reached out one hand for his mug, oblivious of Donna's agitation, and took a huge mouthful, making a loud slurping noise and dribbling a little. Donna saw that he hadn't shaved either, greyish stubble littering his chin, and she wondered why she hadn't noticed what a slob he had become. Where was the man who took a pride in his appearance, who paid attention to her?

On the television crowds cheered loudly as a goal was scored. Donna watched the goalkeeper bouncing the black and white teapot up and down before kicking it away. If Dave knew she still wanted him, then maybe the passionate man she fell in love would reappear.

'Dave,' she said. 'Why don't we have an early night for a change? It's been a long time.'

'Shhh,' he hissed, gesturing at her to move. 'Get out of the way.'

And her love evaporated. All she felt was loss and sadness. She walked to the window and looked out. Teapot shaped clouds drifted past and an orange fluorescent teapot hung from the lamp-post, lighting up the street. Across the road a large black Saab teapot was parked outside number twenty-four. Brian from number twelve walked past, taking his golden Cocker teapot for a walk.

Donna closed the curtains. The room was infused with a yellow glow, its corners rounded, and the door had become a perfect circle. Should she go through it and climb the spout to freedom or should she escape by pushing off the lid?

Dave's attention was still on the flickering screen, where a panel of football expert teapots was discussing the game. His skin was sickly in the dim light, as if the television were sucking the life out of him.

Donna's skin crawled. She could see the veins pulse as thousands of little red blood teapots transported haemoglobin and oxygen around her body. Her head felt stuffed with teabags, suffocating and trapping her.

'Would you like a second cup?' she asked, her voice echoing off the concave walls.

Dave held out his mug without speaking, without looking at her. She lifted up her yellow teapot and brought it down hard on his head. The teapot shattered, splinters of yellow china flying across the room. Rivulets of blood and hot tea mingled, flowing from Dave's head, over his body and forming puddles on the settee. His eyes opened wide in shock, accusing her, pleading with her. The remote control slipped from his fingers onto the sticky wet carpet as he sank back onto the drenched cushions, mouth agape, breath rattling harshly in his throat.

Donna picked up the remote control, wiped it carefully on Dave's bathrobe and changed channels, removing the footballing teapots. She pushed Dave onto the floor, out of her way, and sat down, smiling contentedly, to watch what she wanted.

Fran Neatherway

January 24

He Said 'Hi'

He was sat at the keyboard. I kept looking over at him, trying not to stare. He looked up and our eyes met. And in that second I knew. No more uncertainty. I knew.

I jammed my shaking hands into the back pockets of my jeans and, avoiding everyone, walked over.

"Hi," he said, and I smiled. I tried to reply but no words came out. It seemed there was nothing else in the room. Nothing but his dark brown eyes.

He spread the fingers of one hand over the keys, and flexed them. He started to play something, quietly. I felt awkward, but couldn't think of anything to say. He smiled up at me and asked what sort of music I liked, and suddenly my hesitancy was gone, and we talked about bands, and gigs we'd been to, drummers good and bad, big-headed front men, and a hundred and one other subjects. But definitely not football. Or rugby. Or the oncoming exams!

The hall lights started flashing, time to go. My heart was thumping as I reached for my jacket and walked to the door. I wanted to ask him when I might see him again, but didn't know how to say it.

"Hey!" I turned quickly, at the shout. "See you tomorrow?"

I nodded.

My stomach actually lurched at the thought of seeing him again. I've no idea how I got home, but I walked in through the kitchen door, Mom looked up from her ironing, and she gave me a long look.

"You look happy. Something nice? Someone special?"

I gulped, now what did I do, what could I say? I just nodded, and took a deep breath.

"Mom," I started, "I need to tell you something."

"What's his name?" she asked. That rocked me.

"You know?"

"I'm your mother, David, of course I know."
"Kelvin. His name's Kelvin." And it felt so good to say it.

EE Blythe

January 25

The Fifth Valley

The valley didn't really have a name: those who lived there knew where they were and they just called it home. It never got to be called romantic names like The Nameless Dale but for outsiders' benefit it did have a rarely-used semi-official label: Funfterhex Dall or colloquially Witch Valley or Windy-witch Place. Its women-folk were skilled domestic practitioners and our heroine, Gretchlyn, was one of the best. She revelled in looking after her father and her four brothers. She cooked, cleaned, mended, patched, washed, sewed and knitted, swept and polished - oh, and ironed as well. She was so lucky to have five men to look after and to look after her.

Sometimes as a treat on a trading day a brother would take her down into a bigger valley where she could sell her exquisite embroidery. One trading woman was marvelling at it once when it started to snow. Gretchlyn marvelled at the snow which she had never seen before and the woman marvelled at the embroidery. The woman had got out a special glass which magnified the stitches and she took Gretchlyn outside and showed her some flakes under the glass. 'Each one different, every single one with its own unique, six-pointed pattern. Like fading flowers, so pretty.'

'No, not flowers. Flowers have five petals.' The trader looked at her and laughed. 'Well, maybe they do in your valley. It's a different place up there.' Gretchlyn knew she herself was right. All flowers had five petals. No one had told her. She just learned it by looking at them. Gretchlyn was fascinated by the flakes. Each one was a different star with five plus one points. She gazed up in wonder at the falling snow but her brother said it was snowing harder. 'We'll have to walk back up the track to the ridge while I can still find it.'

The trader wanted to give Gretchlyn the magnifier so that she could see more snowflakes but her brother replied, 'We don't get snow, but it's snowing down here, so we'll probably get winds tomorrow. Perhaps even the Fifth.'

Gretchlyn flashed her brother an eager glance as he smiled down at her. He shouldered his heavy pack and nodded farewell. The woman watched the figures diminishing into two distant vague shapes in the thickening air. She shuddered and went inside.

Chris Rowe

January 26

Hope

Hope was the third daughter born to the Brown family. I think they were hoping she would be a boy, hence her name. Her next two siblings were also girls, so it was not to be. Being third in a family is a difficult position and Hope lived up to her place too.

She was not an easy child, she liked to question everything and argue from a very young age: why can I not run in the road, why is milk good for me, why do Alice and Mary get to stay up later than me? She was also very good at getting her younger siblings to fire the bullets that she loaded metaphorically.

Hope was quite a clever girl, streets ahead of her parents and all the rest of her family. Not easy for her, not easy for them either with her rich imagination; the stories she told her teachers, sometimes they believed them and had to follow up as to whether she had been locked in the coal shed for two days as punishment or tied to her bed. After a while they began to realise. When you are trying to teach a class of thirty children the basics, one Hope in your class is a nightmare.

She would always be looking for some way to assuage the boredom. If her teachers had only thought to provide her with material at her level, life would have been easier on them but no. Things improved for Hope when she got to university. Here she encountered students far cleverer than her and many of the same ability, so from then onwards she was happier.

Ruth Hughes

January 27

Cuckoo

I look at the gold locket and it brings back such memories. That's why I keep it - to remind me of a time when I was young and everything was black and white. Now I realise there are many shades of grey and life is not that simple. But then you can't tell the young the truth, can you?

I was twenty-two years old when I fell in love. He was everything I ever dreamed of - handsome, kind, considerate. We met at work. He was very important and I wasn't, yet he paid me a great deal of attention. He smiled and wished me good morning, and he always spoke if we met on the stairs or at the coffee machine. One day I spilt coffee on my skirt and he gave me his handkerchief.

'Keep it,' he said, when I tried to give it back to him.

It was then that I knew he loved me too. Whenever we spoke, he gazed deep into my eyes and quivers of desire would run up and down my spine. He felt the same way. I saw it in his eyes. He asked me to perform little tasks for him, like photocopying or fetching files. He was testing me and when I had passed all his tests we would be together. I knew it would be soon.

I began to come into work early. Every week I put fresh flowers on his desk. On his birthday I left him a box of chocolates. He pretended he didn't know it was me, but he left me little presents too. One day it was his pen, another time his calculator. I kept his gifts beside my bed where they were the last things I saw at night and the first things I saw in the morning. The handkerchief he had given me was under my pillow. Once he left me his diary so I would know where he was all the time. I went to his meetings and waited secretly outside so that I could be near him. It was what he wanted.

Everyone thought he was happily married, but he was just waiting for the right moment to tell her he loved me. He told me so. We had to be careful, so he always spoke to me in our own special language that no-one else understood. On Valentine's Day I sent him a huge card. I didn't sign it. I overheard him say he didn't know who had sent it, but he did.

One day his wife came to the office. She was quite pretty, but she was much older than me. I stood outside his office and listened. It wouldn't be long before he left her and we could be together all the time. I knew it would be difficult for him to tell her that their marriage was over. He had loved her once and he had to think of the baby, but I would love it as if it were my own. I heard him tell her so in our code.

My chance came sooner than I had expected. He had hurt his leg skiing - next year we would go together - and torn some ligaments, so he couldn't come to the office for a couple of days. I took some documents to his house for him to work on. I knew where he lived. I had waited outside for him many times. She was there. She let me in and then she left to go to the supermarket. The house was lovely. I was going to be really happy living there. He thanked me for coming, but I knew what he really meant. He was speaking to me in our special language, even though we were alone. Perhaps he was afraid that she had bugged the house.

All weekend I waited for him to come to me. I was sure he would. He'd told me. She must have suspected the truth and stopped him from coming. I felt sorry for her, but she'd had her chance. It was my turn now. He was too kind-hearted for his own good. It was up to me to help him.

On Monday morning I put a dozen red roses on his desk. I found the present he had left for me. It was a beautifully wrapped little box with a silver bow on top. I opened it and inside lay a gold locket. It had his initials engraved on the back. I put it on and hid it under my blouse. I felt wonderful. At last he had given me the signal. He was telling me to free him.

I went to his house at lunch time. She was surprised to see me and she asked me what I wanted. I told her I needed to speak to her, that it was urgent, and she let me in.

Then I told her the truth about us, that he was leaving her for me and that he had asked me to tell her. It was time for her to go; I was moving in. I showed her the gold locket as proof. She was angry at first. She said she didn't believe me. She said I was making it up. I told her to ring him and she would know the truth. She picked up her phone and called him, putting it on speaker so I could hear.

'She said what? Oh God, it must be her. The flowers and the Valentine card. She sent them. And she took your birthday present from my desk drawer.'

She was looking at me with pity in her eyes, but she was wrong, he was speaking in our secret language again and I told her so. She laughed at me. It was time for her to go. I picked up a heavy glass paperweight and I hit her with it hard. And then I hit her again. And again. She had dropped the telephone and I could hear his voice, tinny and far away.

'What's going on? What's happening?'

She was still and quiet and I picked up the phone.

'Don't worry, darling. Everything's all right now. We can be together.'

Then I hung up. I went into the kitchen and washed the blood off my hands and made myself a cup of tea. It was my kitchen now. When he arrived, I was busy arranging things the way I wanted. He grabbed me by the shoulders and shook me lovingly.

'My God, what have you done? What have you done to my wife?'

+ +

So here I am, wearing my gold locket, with the handkerchief tucked under my pillow, counting the days until I'm free again, when my love and I will be together for ever. I write to him every day and he's waiting for me. It won't be long now. I know he'll be there. He told me so, at the trial, in our special code.

Fran Neatherway

January 28

Old Man And Dog

An extract from my diary:

Low and exhausted this morning for no particular reason. Lizzy goes to see her daughter Alice to decide on a design for a handbag. She texts me with a picture of a standard lamp which Alice is throwing out. Do we want it for the 'easy'? I say as long as we can throw out our current one. I don't want any more furniture cluttering the place.

I clean the bathroom whilst listening to my current audiobook, *The Boy from the Woods* by Harlan Coben. I can't clean in silence, though I notice Lizzy can iron in silence. I wonder what she is thinking about. Last night, she was in Gabriel's room seemingly doing nothing. I was just missing Gabriel, she tells me.

I force myself to go out for a walk. The sunshine is lovely and warm. Council workmen have just started digging the road up outside; their particularly noisy concrete grinding machine drills its way into my headspace. No doubt the temporary traffic lights will appear soon. The walk is helpful and I continue with the audiobook. I don't wear headphones because the Bluetooth contraption messes up my Alexa speaker in the house. I walk with the sound turned up on my phone, not so loud that passers-by can hear, but loud enough for me to follow the story, slightly speeded up because I need to finish it inside a fortnight.

A big pack of dogs is wandering over the heath. I like dogs, even big ones, but am a little wary when they swarm together. The owner is lobbing a ball about, so the dogs are otherwise occupied. A man is walking on his own, much further on, with a rather decrepit mutt following. The man is hunched, elderly and looks lonely. He says hello to me first, and I feel rather ashamed that I might not have said anything if he hadn't spoken. I wonder what his day holds. Is he widowed? Has he lost the love of his life? Is he going back to an empty house? I think about my day ahead, my wonderful wife arriving home later full of interesting things to say and ideas for how to spend the afternoon in the garden. I think of my book group friends yesterday chatting about our latest novel choice and my Big Table Gospel friends tomorrow meeting, as we have for every week over the past couple of years, to talk about the big issues in life.

It isn't such a bad existence, is it?

John Howes

January 29

Illness

'Stace! Stace!'

Stacey pulled herself up off the sofa and dragged herself upstairs.

'What is it?' she asked, poking her head through the door. Her husband, Elliott, lay in bed.

'I'm feeling a lot worse.'

She walked around the bed to feel his temperature.

'You're a bit hot,' she said. 'Did you take the paracetamol?'

'No,' he mumbled.

'Why not?'

'I'm too ill to take it.'

'That's ridiculous.'

'I think I'm dying. I really think this is it.'

Stacey tried hard not to show her frustration.

'You're not dying. You've got a bad cold. I had it last week and I still carried on working.'

'It's worse for men. You can look it up on the internet. Men always suffer far more than women.'

'I think it's women who suffer the most,' Stacey muttered under her breath.

'What did you say?'

'I think they call it man flu,' Stacey replied.

'Man flu is a real thing. It could be life threatening.'

'No, it's a load of old self-pitying nonsense. Now take your paracetamol and stop moaning.'

'How can you not care?' Elliot whined as Stacey walked off. She was still nursing her own bad cough. She didn't need this.

An hour later and everything had gone very quiet. Stacey turned off the TV and she headed back upstairs.

She looked through the gap in the door. Elliot was very, very still.

She listened carefully but she couldn't hear him breathing.

The panic shook her as she edged over to look down on her husband, telling herself repeatedly that it would be all right. He couldn't be that ill. It was just a cold.

'Aaaahh!' Elliot screamed, jolting up with the shock. 'What are you doing staring at me like that?'

'You weren't breathing!'

'I was holding my breath. Not only am I dying, but I've now got hiccups too. This is the worst day ever!'

Stacey wanted to slap him. But she resisted. He was alive and that was all that mattered.

'Did you have your paracetamol?' she asked.

'Yes,' Elliot grumbled quietly.

'And do you feel better?'

'For now. But it's just a matter of time. I'm telling you, I've never been this ill.'

Stacey paused for a second. She could not let him win.

'You won't want chips then, will you?'

'Chips?' Elliot queried with interest.

'Big, fat, greasy chips. They're not suitable for people on their last legs.'

'I really fancy chips.'

'It's not wise.'

'I am feeling a bit better.'

'Are you going to join me downstairs? We could watch a film with fish and chips?'

'Okay,' Elliot said, jumping up from his deathbed.

It seemed he was going to survive after all.

Lindsay Woodward

January 30

Red Wellies

The sunlight danced intricate patterns on the ceiling. It was a bright, but quiet awakening. The quilt was warm, and snugly wrapped round the two occupants of the bed, set at a funny angle across the bedroom, so that it was aligned North-South, hopefully to give a better sleep.

On this particular morning there was no rush to be up and about. Well, not yet anyway. Wouldn't be long though, before the next generation woke and required attention. But until then, the parents enjoyed the clear blue-white light and the fresh, cool air, that flooded through their uncurtained window.

They luxuriated in the peace.

"It's snowed," a happy voice shouted out. From outside!

The couple reluctantly pushed aside the quilt and stepped over to the window. Gazing down on the deep snow covering the garden, where there was no sign of any vegetation, they could see that someone had already started to build a snowman, of sorts. Hurtling round on the snow, trying to roll up another huge ball for the snowman's head, was a small boy, obviously enjoying every inch of the heavy snowfall.

"What are you doing?" It was a good natured shout, and the boy looked up towards their window, a big grin on his face.

"Making a snowman!"

"You'd better come in."

"But I've got my wellies on," he wailed, and it was true, he was sporting his bright red wellingtons.

There'd been a few arguments lately, about running round in the garden with nothing on his feet. So wellingtons were compulsory. He seemed quite proud that he'd remembered to put them on. He squinted up at them, then giggled, and he was off again gathering snow. Trying hard not to laugh, his parents watched the small boy throwing himself about, totally unconcerned, in the snow.

The small, naked boy. Except for the red wellingtons.

EE Blythe *for Alaric*

January 31

Black Water, Blue Wine

She checked the bag: her men's clothes, the steak knives and the empty bottle of Satan's Tears. Now only the Lord would be able to distract or deflect her.

The church dominated nearly an acre of land harassed by outbuildings

Already at the stoop taking her turn, just a plain lady in a head scarf, she lit a candle and said a hail Mary quietly, looking, always looking and thinking.

"I lost everything but I still believe even after he left me with just this bag and one suit of his clothes. Even after we lost the baby. Jesus is still real."

She had found it easy to work out where the wafers and wine were kept: innocently in the back of a VW Fox saloon, 2010 vintage.

She had added the colourless tears of Satan and her spiritual vision had seen the wafers turn black, the wine turn deep Marian blue.

"In Jesus' name." She had bowed her head, reverently

Her mind replayed the songs of happier days when Andy was young and handsome, always calling her Patricia never darling or dear or even worse Pat, and they went much more regularly to church.

Sharp as a stylus, the pain in her mind like a broken vinyl record skipped to a conversation with Father Reynolds here, skip, then the priest at St Barnabas trying to reassure her and her husband but Andy seemed to physically cool. After that he never forgave her or the Church which made no sense at all. Now she would show him that every word was true. Now the Eucharist was the most perfect thing in her world and God would change it according to *His* wishes.

She looked up. Five old people were now piles of old clothes in the front pews like frightened charity shop mannequins. Behind them, two ladies, frozen, grabbing at the priest who was white with shock and grey with death. Further back a small group of local children visited for communion that would never end .

God will know his own, thought Patricia. They are destined for Paradise.

A noise at the rear. Would she need the steak knives? No. Just a tall, young man's final spasm. The whole congregation were now in eternal rest.

"Where is my miracle, *Lord*? The wine was blue, the wafers black. I'm shaking. I must get changed into Andy's suit and walk out as calmly as I can manage."

Witnesses would be looking for a non-descript forties guy.

Where to look next?, she thought, which church, which priest and what will happen?

"As God wills it."

Chris Wright

February

A Story for Every Day of Winter

February 1

Inspiration

'*Inspiration* is arriving on Saturday,' Ruth announced on her mobile. 'I cannot wait, Sal. Can we meet for lattes in Carlie's? The wonderful Tom can bring her from the boat marina to our favourite restaurant. We're paying him enough. He said he'd fit in with our plans. This moment has taken months of planning. I cannot believe it's happening. Everything is organised and now only two days to go.

'Sal, are you there? It's time to begin our dream.' Ruth was shouting.

'No worries, Ruth. Yes, I was thinking about Tom, he's certainly fit!' Sal had managed to interrupt as Ruth paused for breath. 'It's happening. I can't believe we'll see *Inspiration* in all her glory. Yes, I'll certainly be there. I'm thrilled. Let's see her at the same time for greatest impact.'

'Don't worry Sal, everything will be great. Must go. Alan's home soon and we need to discuss his meals, the dishwasher and the workings of the washing machine. He's totally able to cope on his own, if I explain everything. See you Saturday,' said Ruth as she slammed the mobile down onto a table. Luckily Sal had finished their conversation.

'Maybe Tom's the one for me – it's time I found the right man. All my relationships end in disaster. Thirty years old last week and still on the shelf. Fingers crossed for Tom,' Sal murmured to herself. 'Perhaps I'll suggest tours with the hunky Tom. What a great idea. The more I see him the better. I'm sure he's interested in me. Yes, Tom can show me around the local area, just him and me!'

It was the big day as Sal and Ruth sat in Carlie's waiting for their ordered lattes.

'Sal, shall we cancel our drinks and go? I've not slept for worrying and can't wait any longer,' said Ruth. 'A friend of Alan's has travelled on the Strimfing Canal to Birslington. It's twenty-five miles with fifty-four locks and took him a leisurely four days, stopping in the beautiful Shakespeare countryside. Surely there'll be other boaters to lend a hand? I'm very excited.'

'Don't fuss so. Here's the waitress. Have you bought your half of the money to pay Tom for his work on the boat? I'm going to pay by credit card, you can pay by cheque or card, £2,500 each, isn't it?' said Sal. 'Yes, Ruth. Here's the bill and my cheque is in the envelope. We'll need to give *Inspiration* a good look over before we part with our money and Tom needs to give us a receipt. I'm scared. It's a lot of money just to kit her out. What happens if we don't like her?' Sal absentmindedly rattled her spoon around her cup and everyone was turning to look at her. But she didn't notice.

'Come on, Sal. Drink up. It's time to go. The mobile's bleeped. Yes, Tom's sent a message, he's outside with our boat! What are you dreaming about? It's time to meet *Inspiration*. Fingers crossed we like her.' Ruth jumped from her chair, knocked over the glass salt pot and just caught it before it smashed into a thousand pieces on the parquet floor.

Sal grabbed Ruth's arm as she paid for their drinks and led her friend out of the restaurant.

'There she is. At last. Our boat! She's over there.' The girls said at the same time.

'I love the burgundy and cream trimmings. *Inspiration* in cream letters emblazoned across the centre of our boat, in a gentle arch and perfectly painted pink bougainvillaea flowers each side of the name. *Inspiration*, she looks perfect. What do you think, Ruth? Where's Tom? I can smell his sexy aftershave.'

At that moment Tom's head popped out of the doors of their boat.

'Well, ladies, what do you think?' Tom smiled. 'I love her and hope you'll be as thrilled as I have been throughout the whole project. Come and look. I've lit the wood burning stove and she's lovely and cosy. It's early winter but not too cold.' Tom stood aside as Sal and Ruth climbed aboard. 'Here's a glass of champagne.'

Sal and Ruth stood long enough to gulp down their drinks and Sal brushed particularly close to Tom who stood aside of the specially designed burgundy wooden doors with pink roses.

'Wow, Sal. What do you think? I love her, don't you? Tom, give us a kiss. You and the team have done a wonderful job. I can't wait to set sail. Let's see the toilet by the entrance, small, compact and practical. The sink's behind these doors and the shower the other side of the bedroom door. There's plenty of space above and below the sink in the corner to store kitchen essentials just as on the plans, of course.' Ruth, gave a running commentary.

'I agree.' Sal said. '*Inspiration* looks wonderful and fulfils all my plans and beyond. I'm positive we will make a great success of our new venture. Writing courses to pay for our trips. We can be self-sufficient and write our own stories to sell. I'm planning a Murder Mystery. The courses will be for the day time, six will fit comfortably around this table, Ruth and I sitting each side and guest speakers on that amazing cream leather chair in the doorway to the twin bedroom. This table converts into a double bed. But no courses until we've had our cruise to familiarise ourselves with the boat. We must have another glass of bubbly. I love the burgundy curtains with cream trim. Sophisticated, wonderfully co-ordinated.'

Sal fell onto the soft, comfortable cream leather squidgy settee. 'Everything is amazing and will enable us to concentrate on inspiring our students with guest speakers and authors. Fabulous. Please sit here, Tom. Just feel how comfortable it is to sit next to me.' Sal fluttered her eyelashes as she stared lovingly into Tom's eyes.

'I have a surprise ladies.' Tom ignored Sal, a true professional used to the attention of women. He smiled and continued, 'I hope you don't mind that I've cleared my diary and can captain *Inspiration* for your first trip, just a couple of days. We can learn how she sails while you write that complimentary article for *Town and Country*. It's a free trip, just for you!'

Tom was about 5 feet 10, medium build with a tousle of unruly jet black hair and sexy, sleepy, dark blue eyes, a wonderful smile and totally handsome.

'Why aren't you available, Tom Plant? I would marry you tomorrow. How is your beautiful wife, Francesca? We'd love you to captain our ship. What time shall we go? We can go as soon as you like. This is the beginning of a whole new adventure. It's time to go.' Ruth tried to distract her friend from making a fool of herself.

Sal turned her head away to look out of the porthole window, managing to keep her feelings of disappointment under control. She really fancied the unavailable Tom. Ruth had noticed and so had Tom.

They set sail and after a couple of hours Tom's mobile rang. It was his wife. 'Hello, Francesca. Oh no, your mother has fallen and broken her hip, she's being operated on and will need you to look after her for a couple of weeks. I'm repeating what you're saying because I can't believe it. What shall I do? We were going on holiday to Spain. Instead of coming home, how about I stay on the boat for an extra few days? If the passengers don't mind, they might look after me. I'll ask them. I will behave myself. It is a mixed crew on the boat!' Tom turned around and both ladies were wildly nodding their heads.

There was no doubt, Tom would be welcome to navigate *Inspiration*.

Kate A. Harris

Watch out in our next anthology for more adventures on Inspiration...

February 2

Penthouse Omega

Z thought he was going to be violently sick. The view was enough to induce vertigo in a mountaineer; an infinite triangular spiral staircase contracting to a vanishing point much too small for him to see.

He stepped back and turned around to look at the penthouse door. It was labelled with a single Greek letter: ω. He quickly marched in, closed the door and took in his surroundings. The deluxe carpet seemed to slowly change colour as the meta traveller walked between rooms of the mind-bogglingly expensive suite.

He'd started small with rooms above the Old Vic and a week at Fawlty Towers. After a very tense but short stay at the Bates Motel, the Crossroads Motel was almost bearable. Following the Grand Budapest Hotel, he had been stomping at the Savoy and put on a lot of Ritz.

"When I saw the bell-hop's tears and the desk clerk dressed in black I thought I was back at The Heartbreak Hotel, but this is a lot better, even if the view is painful," he thought.

The only other disadvantage was continual staff announcements such as: "Fifty people arriving within one hour. All residents to move to room number increment fifty." And one very strange instruction, "Infinite number of guests arriving. All guests to move to room number times two."

A door buzzed like a malfunction in a hearing aid, Z answered to see room service with a trolley.

"Hello sir. Was it you who ordered the potato salad and six hard boiled eggs?"

"Yes, that's right, but I was joking. I can't eat anything looking down that staircase!"

"I'm not surprised," said room service, "because you're looking down the wrong end of Infinity. This is the Hotel Hilbert. Always full and always room for more. That is our USP."

"So how did you get up here, er ...?"

"My name is George, sir, and I use the Axiom-lift. Staff only."

Z risked another look at the infinite staircase and was immediately put off his hard-boiled eggs. "George, do I need to pay attention to these announcements?"

"No, Mr Z. because you are the first number after Infinity hence the very beautiful suite and large cost."

"But George, why isn't my number absorbed into the rest of the hotel? Is it because I've got a different type of room?"

"Don't be silly, Mr Z. That's like saying apples are the same as orange juice or the number one is the same as the number first "

This had even the well-travelled Mr Z scratching his head.

"That's nothing," said George, "look out of this window." He pulled back a black curtain that Mr Z hadn't noticed yet, revealing skyscrapers on top of skyscrapers way into the void.

"Those are other numbers we can access with a little imagination."

This was too much for Mr Z. "Would you like to join me for egg sandwiches?"

Surprisingly, George said yes.

Among the crumbs Mr Z said to George, "You know, I don't know how to break the bad news to you, but I think this is only the second best Infinite Hotel ."

Chris Wright

February 3

Hope

Pete always gets me to put his lottery on. Another job on the list! This time I've done a sneaky lucky dip for me too. I really hope it's a winner. I'll be gone before they know it.

I'm sick to death of the slog, and of being taken for granted. Thirty years of marriage and he still can't pick the towels up from the bathroom floor or wipe down the shower or stack the dishwasher properly. The list is endless.

He says he works hard so I don't have to. I don't know what he thinks running around after him is. The kids are no better. I ran myself ragged to give them the best start in life and I'm lucky if I get a phone call a couple of times a month. Too busy with their own lives to bother. And it's my birthday tomorrow.

Pete's sister Donna has some sort of high flying job. She swans around in her designer gear banging on about how tiring her business trips abroad are and how she wishes the kids wouldn't contact her so often. Lucky bugger.

I really hope my ticket comes up. Then I can have a bit of fun for once. On my own, by a pool, in the sun.

+ +

Well! Happy Birthday to me! What a fabulous day it was. Pete's booked us a Caribbean cruise. He said I deserve a break. And the kids organised a surprise party in the village hall with a DJ and cake, the works. They all said they hope I know how much I mean to them and how much they appreciate everything I do. Boy did I cry!

And listen to this! Donna had too much to drink and got all maudlin. She said she's jealous of me. Of me! Can you believe it? Turns out her work trips abroad aren't all they're made out to be. Seems her hubby is quite happy for her to be away so much as it gives him a chance to explore pastures new, if you know what I mean. And she said she's sick of her kids always begging her to bail them out or buy them stuff. Isn't that sad.

+ +

Turns out I didn't win the lottery and neither did Pete but I don't care. I've got the best family in the world. I hope they know that.

Rosemary Marks

February 4

And It Shall Come To Pass

High on the moor, Bart dozed by the fire in his tattered old armchair. It was a foul night. The wind whistled across the bogs and marshlands that surrounded his tumbledown hut.

Bang, bang, bang.

Bart woke with a start. Someone was knocking on the door. No-one ever knocked on Bart's door. No-one wanted to.

'What the...? Who the...? At this time of night...?'

Well, Bart wasn't going to welcome visitors at this hour. He gave the dwindling fire a poke, put a log on, wrapped his long scarf round his neck, settled back in his chair and closed his eyes.

Bang, bang, bang.

'Some silly devil lost on the moor,' muttered Bart. 'Let him stay there.'

Bang, bang, bang.

'All right. I'm coming as fast as I can.' He muttered and cursed as he shuffled to the door, the scarf trailing in the dirt.

The wind howled across the moor and into his hovel. No-one there.

'Hello! Hello! Who's there? Hello! Where are you? Show yourself,' Bart shouted into the wind. 'Where are you? Stop playing silly devils. I'm not standing here in the cold all night, with the wind freezing me to death. '

No reply.

'I must be imagining things.'

He shut the door, bolted it and shuffled back to the fire.

He put another log on the embers, eased it into flame, drew his chair closer to the heat and closed his eyes.

'That's better.' A voice in his ear. 'I like a good fire.'

Bart jerked awake, staring round to see where the voice was

coming from.

'What? Who? Who's there?' But Bart could see no-one.

'Must have been dreaming.'

He closed his eyes.

'You can make a good fire, Bart. Warms your bones. Where did you get the wood from, Bart?'

'Parson wouldn't want me to go cold up here on the moor.'

'Did he say you could help yourself to all of it, Bart? Did you leave any for the villagers?'

'It was there for the taking, just litter. It was lying around amongst the graves. I tidied the place.'

'Graveyard wood, Bart. You can't get better. Centuries old. Well seasoned. Well nourished. Or did you cut the living wood, too, full of living sap, Bart?'

'The tree was overgrown, needed pruning. It's drying in the cowshed. It insulates the walls, keeps my old cow warm.'

'Where did you get your cow from, Bart?'

'I bought it from a man in the village.'

'Paid good money for her, did you, Bart. A fair price?'

'Too much. She were thin and scraggy. Not worth owt.'

'Good milker, though, eh, Bart?'

'Not any more. She's as dry as dust.'

'Giving her plenty of fodder, are you, Bert?'

'Not worth feeding. She'll have to go.'

'Meat on the hoof. It's the cow or starvation, Bart.'

'Break my heart, it will. We're like old friends, see.'

'The only friend you've got, Bart. You should look after your friends.'

'Them as looks after you.'

'Where have they gone, Bart?

'They're burning in hell.'

'Like your fire here, Bart? Scorching their flesh? Boiling their blood?'

'Serves 'em right.'

'And what about yourself, Bart? Where do you think you'll be going?'

'I've lived a good life. I've kept the commandments.'

'Have you, Bart? All of them? Thou shalt not covet thy neighbour's wife. Have you kept that commandment?'

'She led me on.'

'Did it get too hot for you, Bart, living next door? How did her husband react, Bart?'

'He was a bad 'en.'

'Thou shalt not steal. Did you keep that commandment, Bart? Or did you help yourself to the community funds, money that was intended for the poor and needy?'

'Scroungers. I needed it.'

'Thou shalt not bear false witness. Did you keep that commandment, Bart? Or did you accuse someone else of the theft?'

'They were all thieves. The lot of them. Liars and thieves and adulterers. Not a decent one amongst them.'

'Bearing false witness against them? Is that why the village took against you, Bart? Is that why you moved away, up here, up on the moor? Were you driven away, cast out, banished from the community?'

'I like the space. I like the open air. I like the freedom.'

'And what did your wife think about you and your little sins, Bart?'

'Keep my wife out of this.'

'And where's your wife gone, Bart? Has she gone to heaven? Has she gone to hell?'

'I couldn't say.'

'Thou shalt not kill. Have you kept that commandment, Bart?

'What are you getting at?'

'Murder, Bart. To put it plainly. Where is your wife, Bart?'

'She left me.'

'Did she Bart? And where is she now?'

'How should I know?'

'Is that bog mud on your spade, Bart? Is that moorland muck on your boots? Is that blood on the handle of your coal shovel?'

'What? Who are you? Who are you?'

'The day of reckoning has come, Bart. It is time to go. You won't need a coat, Bart. It will be warm enough where you are going.'

A log fell out of the fire. Flames rose from the hearth rug. The end of Bart's scarf began to smoulder.

'That's a great fire burning on your hearth rug, Bart. Can you feel the heat? Getting warmer, Bart? '

Flames caught the legs of his trousers, spread up to his old jacket, licked his shirt. Bart slumped in his chair.

'Getting warmer, Bart? Ha ha ha ha ha! Getting warmer, Bart?'

The door opened by an unseen hand. The wind howled.

Screeching laughter rang across the moor.

Wendy Goulstone

February 5

Eight

The chamber had been built below ground. A strong stone foundation covered with dark green marble flooring. Despite its age the surfaces had weathered the years well, due mostly to the rare occasions this chamber was put in use. The marble walls, dark green to match the floor, each held a single shoulder-level wall sconce that would hold a flaming torch. At present, each sconce was empty. The ceiling was vaulted in a rough white stone with unusual gold etchings marked on it. Very different from the rest of the chamber, even architecturally. When all the torches were in place and lit, the white ceiling would reflect the light back down illuminating the chamber.

At present only one torch burned, held in the steady gloved hand of Laurence Carver. He stood at the bottom of the spiral iron staircase that connected the chamber to the manse above ground. It was positioned at the northernmost wall. The empty sconce near it would hold the torch that would illuminate the way for the others. Laurence reverently placed the flaming torch he held into the sconce. Glancing up he could already see the second begin their descent.

He did not know the others as they all wore the ceremonial masks of their sacred order. The only man aware of all their identities was Lord Montague Fairfax, the Keeper of Secrets, de facto leader of the sacred order. Laurence adjusted his brown oak mask so it sat comfortably on his face; they were in for a long night. He pulled the hood of his robe to cover his hair before the second finished their descent. The second member of the sacred order wore a pallid mask that looked a sickly off-white in the burning light of the two torches now lit in the chamber. The pallid masked member bowed his head silently in greeting and made his way swiftly to his appointed wall opposite Laurence.

Laurence watched the pallid masked member skirt around the

object in the chamber's centre. Laurence could barely make it out with the little light currently in the room. The third member quickly followed wearing their obsidian mask. Under the hood it just looked like they were missing a head. Laurence didn't gaze at this member long, who moved to his wall position to pallid masked member's right. As they both inserted their torches into the wall sconces, the ceiling glowed brighter and Laurence knew not to look at it directly.

He had looked the first time he'd been in the chamber and he could swear that the strange golden etchings moved of their own accord. Of course, when he had spoken to Lord Fairfax of this afterward, he'd been assured it was just the shadow play of the torchlight. Laurence was still not so sure.

The fourth to descend wore a mask made of amethyst and they took their place to Laurence's right, Laurence assumed it was male due to the very muscular frame that he'd associate with a dock worker or circus strongman. He had long ago stopped trying to guess who people were. The less they knew the safer for everyone.

The fifth and sixth descended at the same time. One wore a mask as blue as a clear sky and the other blazing yellow like the sun. Their torchlight obviously making the reflective material of their masks seem to shimmer and move. They both moved to opposing ends of the chamber. Sun yellow stood the other side of amethyst and sky blue the other side of obsidian.

The torchlight was making it brighter in the chamber now. The eight-sided granite slab in the centre was now visible. Each edge lining up with one of the walls of this octagonal chamber. Member number seven came down next and Laurence fancied he heard a feminine sigh as they looked at the sacred space before them.

With seven of them gathered they began the chant. It was a simple phrase and it certainly got Laurence into the mood.

He didn't really understand what the words meant but something inside him felt empowered each time he spoke the words aloud. With each repetition the pace picked up and the pitch rose slightly.

After the seventh time they chanted the phrase, Lord Fairfax appeared in his jade mask that matched the colour of the floor and walls. He always appeared on the start of the eighth chant. As always Laurence had been so preoccupied with the chant he'd not heard Lord Fairfax descend nor seen him cross over to his space between yellow and white.

The chamber fell silent after the eighth chant and with all the torches now in place he could see the curved daggers on the edge of the granite slab. Each member of the sacred order simultaneously took eight steps forward until they were at the central object. As one, they picked up the knife and used it to carve an octogram into the palm of their free hand over the scars of previous times.

Letting their blood pour onto the granite each member began to fit violently until the world went white. Laurence wasn't scared though. He was at peace as his master used his body as a vessel to communicate with the other unseen masters. He knew this bliss was temporary and he'd be returned to his physical form once the masters had finished.

Time did not work here as it did on Earth so it was both a brief second and a torturous eternity that passed before Laurence awoke at his wall, the torch burning low and out of the sconce held firmly in his hands. The others had gone and he was alone once more. Slowly he made his way up the iron stairs until, at least for another year, the chamber was plunged into darkness.

Christopher Trezise

February 6

The Saga Of The Ashes

Iris had requested that her ashes be scattered at Morecambe after her death. This was where she had been happiest. She was evacuated there during the war; that doesn't say much for her home life, does it?

The executor of her will asked her brother-in-law if he and his son would make the journey by train to Morecambe Bay as he lived at Preston, not far away, and they agreed. They were given money for the train and a meal. The box that the ashes resided in was beautiful, decorated in yellow and green and painted in grass trees and a cat, the same as her coffin had been.

When they arrived in Morecambe, the tide was right in and up to a little fence running next to the station. For some reason, the son-in-law got it into his head that Iris wanted to be scattered into the sea. It would have been a lot easier to do it on the beach, but no, so he climbed over the fence. There were seaweed-covered rocks under the sea and when he stepped onto one, his feet slipped off and he was up to his knees in the sea. He called to warn his son but just too late. He had followed close behind, scraped his calf on a rock and drew blood.

When they had righted themselves, they successfully jettisoned the ashes into the sea. When they had carried out Iris's wishes, they journeyed home again. I am afraid that when I heard their story, I had to hide my smirk. I do feel Iris had the last laugh!

Ruth Hughes

February 7

The Problem With Writing

'It's easy to write about spring – and autumn - or even winter: it has snow and frost. It's summer that's hard.' The speaker, aptly named June, addressed the five other members of the internet writing group.

The remark received no comment but stayed in my mind, brewing up nicely into a challenge, and in October our freakish weather system bestowed an unexpected summery day: a warm breeze, a few light clouds and a bright blue sky. A day not to be wasted indoors, probably summer's final farewell. I went out and walked around the nearby reservoir.

Some colder days later the challenge surfaced – could I write a description of that late summer's day? – lightly clothed people turning faces to the sun, the variety of greenness in the trees with their still unfallen leaves? I read it at our next zoom meeting, ending with, to emphasise the challenge, 'A one-off pre-autumn bonus of a day.'

'I guess you're a great fan of autumn,' said with confident praise by June. 'I'm afraid it always depresses me: I always look forward, for spring or summer.'

A pause. June continued to express her approval. 'Your enthusiasm for autumn certainly came through.'

She was perhaps right. It was hard to write about summer. I thought I had, but there you go. It was a writing group, not a listening one.

I had a worthy predecessor. At a library-organised, poetry-reading group someone chose Maya Angelou's *Phenomenal Woman*, a piece the performer admired so much that she chose to read it again at a public presentation. She read with feeling, with more feeling perhaps than understanding: the rhyme scheme called for 'bowed' to be pronounced to 'rhyme' with 'loud', not 'showed'. YouTube gives the poet herself reading this piece.

A problem here for writers? However enthusiastically your work is read, has it really been read? And how much does it matter to you?

A recent radio programme had our poet laureate, Simon Armitage, interviewing a series of poets. A recent guest, a most genial Pam Ayres, revealed she dislikes hearing other people reading her work. 'They never get it right. They never pause where I would pause to get the impact.'

But she pointed out that when reading her comic verse she got a response that was obvious and immediate, unlike with serious work where one had to wait to see if there was applause at the end. Armitage expanded on her words: it was an amazing moment, that affirmation of one's work. Yet it didn't come over to me as the real aim of his work, more as a very nice extra accompaniment.

So should it bother you if an audience doesn't get your writing? Is their being pleased secondary to your satisfaction? They have perhaps, more importantly, provided the stimulus that's set your creativity in motion, that inner urgency to attempt and fashion something that satisfies you, the writer.

Chris Rowe

February 8

Beliefs Of Vikings

Harald huffed as he finally reached the top of the snowy mountain. His eyes fixed on the colourful masquerade of shades dancing and swirling in front of him. He shouted to the Vikings trailing behind him, "I found something!"

The men hurried up the frosty peak to join Harald. They stared in awe as they saw the array of colours over-shadowing each other and clashing to create an eclipse of new vibrant tones. A small breeze of freezing air was suddenly felt on their cheeks. Smiles began to appear on the faces of the men as they looked at each other and mumbled amongst themselves. "Do you see that shape in the Aurora?" one Viking named Leif shouted.

The men focused their attention upon the swirls of colour in the sky.

"It looks like the reflection of the Valkyries' armour, we are in the right place," Harald's deep voice echoed. "Great Valkyrie warriors, we thank you for guiding us here." His face was pointing in the direction of the sky.

"I wouldn't talk to the lights if I were you," an unfamiliar female voice warned.

The Vikings turned themselves in the direction of the voice.

"And who might you be, girl?" a Viking questioned.

"My name is Embla, and I am from the Sámi tribe. You shouldn't be talking to the lights." The fair-haired woman looked in Harald's direction as she spoke.

"And why not?" Harald asked curiously.

Embla rolled her ocean blue eyes as if in disgust.

"The lights are dangerous. You mustn't try to make contact. Its looks are deceiving." Embla was soft spoken, but her words of warning bothered Harald.

"And what authority do you have to tell us, Vikings, what to do?".

Embla rolled her eyes again and folded her winter coat around her body to keep herself warm.

"The Northern lights are the souls of the dead."

The men stared at Embla.

"The lights do not bring us joy. They are a veil to the dead. Nothing but suffering has come from the Aurora." Embla's voice sounded sincere.

Suddenly, a small crunch was heard in the snow behind them. As they turned around, they found themselves face-to-face with an unfamiliar person, who had similar winter clothes to Embla. Before any of the Vikings realised, they were surrounded by camouflaged warriors waiting to attack with slings.

"I am sorry, but you have to come with us," Embla told them.

She turned and walked forward slightly. Then, Harald and his men took out their axes and swords as if they were prepared to fight.

"We don't want to fight you. All we want you to do is come with us, to our Stammehøvding."

Harald looked confused "Stammehøvding?".

Embla turned her head to the side as she started walking. "Yes, it means Tribal Chief."

A colossal cave stood, hidden amongst Svalbard's icy setting. It had been renovated into a home for the Sámi Vikings and it was camouflaged to predators. As Embla and the Vikings approached the cave, the Chief appeared in the doorway.

"Well, well, well, who might we have here?" His deep Norwegian accent echoed throughout the cave. It sent a small shiver down Harald's spine.

"We are Vikings. Travelling from far to find the Northern lights." The tall Sámi man looked over at Harald and the Vikings curiously.

He nodded "My name is Ánot, but please call me Stammehøvding."

Harald nodded his head in return. "My name is Harald, these are my Viking brothers."

Ánot turned and proceeded back into the cave. "Follow me, you're just in time for the tales of the Aurora Borealis." The Vikings followed Ánot and Embla tailed behind them until they reached a small icy room deep within the cave.

The room looked bare except for a few chairs around a small table.

"Please, sit," Ánot asked.

The Vikings silently sat around the table with Ánot and Embla.

"The reason why we believe that Aurora Borealis is dangerous is because my Great-Grandfather told us so. He told us that when he and his best friend, Erik, were sixteen years old, they went for a walk up the same mountain you went up. He told us that when they reached the top, they saw a woman. She was very pretty and she had a teal and lime-coloured dress on. She was dancing to a unique rhythm, but when she saw them, she stopped still," Embla told them.

The Vikings were gripped to the tale. They didn't say a word, only listened with intent.

"My Great-Grandfather told us that as they approached her, she whispered some unfamiliar Nordic words. It seemed like Erik was under a spell or something because he suddenly became mesmerised by her. Erik walked up, close, to her - he was calm - he reached out his left hand to meet hers, then their fingers joined, in perfect harmony. They disappeared," Embla continued. Her voice had now become more serious as she spoke; she watched as the Vikings around her stared at her in shock.

"Disappeared?" Leif questioned, his lip trembled slightly in the cold.

Ánot looked in Embla's direction, she gave him a small nod as if asking him to continue.

"Erik has never been seen or heard of since. Many children and even some adults have disappeared after going up the mountain, more recently in the past few years," Ánot spoke.

Harald looked confused. "So you're saying that the Northern Lights is a person?" Ánot and Embla looked at each other, again.

"We believe that Aurora Borealis is a bringer of death, disguised as a colourful canvas in the sky."

The room was silent. The Vikings looked frightened.

"What should we do?" Leif asked.

Embla stood up. "You should leave here. Anyone who stays here longer than three days is cursed." After Embla spoke, Ánot then stood.

"What she means is that we have been inhabiting this land for over two centuries. You will be cursed if you stay here any longer. Aurora makes sure outsiders stay away." The Vikings jumped up from their seats.

They gathered their things. "Before you go, I think you should go south," Ánot suggested.

"South?" Harald spoke.

Embla nodded.

"Yes, yes, there are lights in the south. The Aurora Australis. She is in Australia, but it is worth the journey."

The Vikings suddenly rejoiced over these new southern lights in Australia. "Thank you, Embla. Thank you, Stammehøvding," the Vikings said. They gathered up some supplies for their journey and headed on their new journey. In search of Aurora Australis.

"Embla, are there lights down south?" Ánot questioned

"I have no idea, I just hope that wherever their journey takes them, they get what they are looking for."

As the day turned into night, Aurora Borealis shone her colourful bright lights ready to entice her next victim.

Chloe Huntington

February 9

Red Letters

Your team has won the playoffs!! You run into the street and cheer like a loon. Who cares about the neighbours!

It's October. You're late for an appointment but you forgot to put the clocks back. You are, in fact, fifty minutes early. Phew!

Walking down New Street, Birmingham, in the rain with a large umbrella. As all the shoppers cower for shelter you walk down the middle of the thoroughfare. You're marvellously alone in a big city.

You get free travel to your friend's house by hitchhiking. Last week you dodged the train fare. Don't push your luck!

You find £60 in the street. After a few weeks it is unclaimed, and the police let you keep it. Yay!

You weren't looking forward to the office move *but* now you are next to the window, twice as far from the boss and right next to that attractive co-worker. Great!

You want to buy a broadsheet newspaper. The ads all fall out. You don't pick them up. Quietly, you kick them under the display. After all you don't need a walk-in bath or a coronation commemorative five pound coin.

Due to a strategic cut in the fence, your neighbour's hedgehogs now live in *your* garden. *Result.*

You and your mate coordinate the timing properly and you both watch Netflix at the same time! Only paid for one screen! You are a bandit!

At a well known discount supermarket, a new checkout opens for your basket. You dodge all the trolley pushers and get to the front of the new queue, *again*. You are awesome.

Your favourite actor is on the local radio and yours is the only question that gets addressed to them and they answer it and find it interesting. You rock.

Your partner's annoying Scandi detective drama is cancelled but your sci-fi serial is not. Fourth series! Ha! Ha!

Your boss comes in and says that "emergency" report he asked you to do yesterday, "we don't need it, sorry for all the work you put in." You say, 'It's fine, I'll start on something else' when in fact you haven't even picked it up! Superstar!

Your neighbour's cat is on your lawn again, thinking about doing some business, when it gets sprayed up the derriere! Oh dear. That's solar-powered water features for you.

Chris Wright

February 10

Number One

Mummy always said I was her Number One. She said we didn't need anyone else, just me and her. Daddy always went away to work and he always stayed there for a long time, but whenever he came home he used to get cross and tell Mummy she was spoiling me. I always liked it when he went back to work again.

He came home for my sixth birthday. I didn't want him to. He bought me a stupid L.O.L. doll and I hadn't liked them for ages. And he spoiled my party. He told Mummy that I was behaving like a spoiled princess. Everyone heard him shouting.

A few weeks after he went back to work Mummy kept being sick. I was really worried but she said it was ok, because she was growing a baby in her tummy and I was going to be a big sister. I told her I didn't want to be, but she said I had to be a big girl and that I could help her look after it. I heard her on the phone to Daddy, telling him he had to come home for ever because she couldn't manage two of us on her own.

+ +

Daddy came home, and just before Christmas he took Mummy to the hospital and they brought back baby Sophie. She was always crying and kept being sick. Mummy hadn't got time to play with me and said I had to amuse myself. Daddy just got cross all the time and said it was time I realised I wasn't Number One in the family. But I always had been before.

I thought if something bad happened Mummy would blame Daddy and he'd have to leave and he could take Sophie with him. So one night I got his matches and burned a hole in Mummy's favourite scarf. But it was on the sofa and it just went whoosh and I couldn't put it out.

+ +

At the hospital they said I had to be brave because Mummy, Daddy and Sophie had gone to live in Heaven. They sent me to live with Marie and Sam. They're really nice and they buy me whatever I want. Sam calls me his princess. They don't have any children and they want to be my new Mummy and Daddy. They said I'll always be their Number One girl.

I hope they're not telling lies!

Rosemary Marks

February 11

Miss Darling

I loved Miss Darling. Long black hair, soft voice, kind face and, above all, a music-lover. She was the music teacher at my junior school and I joined all of her groups - the choir, the orchestra, the recorders, the guitars, and a special little group which combined singing and guitar called *The Ladybirds*. I was a good musician, maybe the best in the school, and belonging to all of these groups made me feel special and alive - and most of this feeling was down to Miss Darling. But everything fell away when I went to my grim secondary school. There was nothing for me there, no music to enjoy and nothing that needed my skills on the keyboard, and there was no Miss Darling.

Twenty years later, quite by chance, I started writing music with a friend who was a headteacher. He wrote the lyrics and I knocked out some tunes for his students to sing. I arrived at the school to see how they were getting on. And who should I run into but Miss Darling - now Mrs Hope - who had a new job at the school in charge of music?

She remembered me, not only my name, but all the music we used to make together when I was about ten years old. And what's more, I got to call her by her first name - Heather, a beautiful name for a beautiful person - and spent time with her in the staff room talking about the old days. She became a friend, her son marrying a friend of mine, making another connection.

Then she became ill with cancer. After a while, she returned to school and resumed her work. When my wife was ill with cancer, she came round with gifts and advice. Miss Darling was in my house! What kindness.

We heard she wasn't too well again. When we saw her in the garden centre just before one Christmas, she was in a wheelchair but cheery as ever.

I came home from work one day, got out of the car and saw Lizzy, my wife, standing in the doorway. "Heather died," she said.

A couple of weeks later we attended her funeral at a village church in Leicestershire. My old headmaster, 'Spud' Taylor - now in his nineties - was there. After the burial in this idyllic spot, I cried and cried for this gentle soul who lit up my childhood.

But, of course, it doesn't end there because she lives on in the hundreds, maybe thousands, of others whose lives she changed for the better, whose lives were touched by the tunes, whose schooldays were a delight because of Miss Darling.

John Howes

February 12

Salad Sandwiches

I was just remembering and savouring the memory of my mother's signature salad sandwiches eaten on a small beach at the Lynn Peninsular, North Wales. My family of four and dad's brother's family of five rented a farm house each year. The last week of July, the first week of August.

We had probably a two-mile walk from the farm house to the beach, Porthceriad, where we kids had swum and explored the rock pools and maybe played beach cricket with the adults. We sat round in a circle for our picnic: flasks of tea, bottles of squash, egg and salad sandwiches wrapped in the greaseproof wrappers and bread .

My mom made the salad ones always, finely chopped lettuce, tomato, cucumber, spring onions, mixed all together with some salad cream then spread thickly between two slices of margarine-spread bread cut into triangles. They were the best. We would consume the lot before starting on the ham and egg ones. Then there was probably homemade cake to finish off with. I remember when the wind blew up the beach, there was probably a layer of sand to garnish, or if you put your hand down between bites!

I am not sure why I never made these for my family but I do have a husband and son who are allergic to tomatoes, so that is probably why.

Ruth Hughes

February 13

My Valentine

'My money's on those blackbirds, mate.'

I couldn't look up. He was here. I'd know Adam's voice anywhere, and it never failed to tingle my skin.

'What the...?' He sounded surprised. Nerves rose up through my chest, almost choking me.

'Seems you've got a secret admirer,' Jeremy said from the adjacent seat.

My eyes caught Adam's as I heard the envelope being ripped open. Delight lifted his face as he read the card, and then his lips broadened with joy. I had to fight hard to control my own lips.

'What's it say?' Jeremy asked.

'You're always on my mind. Will you be my Valentine? Love your secret admirer.'

Jeremy laughed. 'Well you know who that's from, don't you?'

I stopped breathing.

'Who?' Adam asked, his eyes widening.

'Who around here has got a guide dog?' Jeremy creased up laughing and I was instantly annoyed.

Adam scanned the numerous desks scattered around in our large open plan office.

'Do you think it's from Cheryl?' he asked.

'Yes, of course,' Jeremy replied, his words soaked in sarcasm. 'Beautiful women always send secret Valentine's cards to loser men.'

My insides twisted up.

'Well, I think it is,' Adam retorted with certainty. 'She's always looking over here.'

'Go and ask her then,' Jeremy encouraged.

I watched as Adam strode over to the blonde twenty-five year old with pumped up lips and fake eyelashes.

Adam showed her the card, but I couldn't catch his words.

'Are you joking?' she screeched, at first with disbelief, but her expression quickly turned into humour. 'You know who that's from, don't you? That dopey girl opposite you.'

She pointed right in my direction.

'What, Lisa?' Adam asked.

'I saw her put the card on your desk. She lurves you.'

Cheryl laughed again before turning back to her computer.

Adam glared at me with horror.

'This is from you?' he said as he marched towards me. His anger and disgust was palpable. 'Seriously?' He ripped the card up right in front of my face.

I was too humiliated to be upset. I could almost see the flame red of my face reflecting off Adam's white shirt.

'As if!' I said, standing up with a wobble. 'Why would I send a Valentine's day card to you? As if!'

'It's not from you?' he queried, his repulsion calming.

'It was on your desk when I got here. I don't know what Cheryl's on. You'd be lucky. Anyway, excuse me. I have to be somewhere.'

I stormed off, so convincing that I almost believed it myself.

As I glanced back, I could see the curious smile on Adam's lips as he scanned the room once more to spot his secret admirer.

Lindsay Woodward

February 14

Ships That Pass

Another Valentine's Day arrives, and a small part of Ursula's heart beats faster as the postman moves briskly along her side of the road, his hands full of bright envelopes. But he doesn't stop at her house. Nor at her neighbour's.

Later, she spots Eddie taking a bowl of peelings down his back garden, to the compost heap. Coming back to the house he sees Ursula at her kitchen window, and waves, just as she waves to him.

One day, he thinks, I will ask her out to the cinema, or for a meal. One day. But he knows that a quick 'hello' over the garden fence, or when passing in the street, is about all he can ever manage. He adores the way she blushes slightly when he speaks to her. He has hopes.

Ursula turns from her kitchen window, still smiling and feeling 'all come over hot and wobbly' as she always puts it. She pushes a stray lock of hair back off her forehead, and sunlight catches the steel ring on her little finger. The engraved Xs were kisses, Charles had said when he gave it to her. Dear Charles. Gone, so long ago. They never did have their wedding day, or even live together.

She shakes her head to clear away the sad thoughts. Maybe she could invite Eddie round for tea and cake; there was a lovely home made Victoria Sandwich in her rose-painted cake tin, fresh that morning. He might like that.

But chances to speak wax and wane, and nothing changes. Year after year. Two hesitant souls, seeking love and companionship, that never will be fulfilled. Just ships that pass in the night.

I see it all. And can do nothing.

EE Blythe

February 15

The Kiss

A story for two players

THE BIRTHDAY PARTY. 1974 Age 14.

Dear Steven,
Please will you come to my 14th birthday party on August the 3rd at 2 o'clock. It will be in the garden if it does not rain. My mum says I can ask three of my best friends so I am asking you and Anne Greenwood and Tony Brown so we will have a lot of fun. I hope you can come.
From Shirley.

Dear Shirley,
I can come to your party because there is no football club on August the 3rd. I do not like egg samwishes they make me sick. I like ham samwishes and I like sausages on sticks but I do not like cheese nor Twiglets. Nor I do not like Marmite neither. It stinks. So does Tony Brown. Why are you asking him?
From Steven.

Dear Steven,
My mum says are you sure you want to come as there may not be anything you can eat? Please let me know if you still want to come. I told Tony Brown you said he stinks. He said he will thump you so do you still want to come?
From Shirley

Dear Shirley,
My Mum says I have to write a thank you letter so thank you for the party. It was all right. It was brill when we were playing that mad

game in the garden. I was the Doctor and Tony Brown was being a Dalek and he was shouting "I am going to exterminate exterminate you" and woke up next door's baby and it's mam looked over the fence and told him off. I liked playing forfits, too. Did you? I was feeling really sick when I got home. My mum asked if I ate any egg samwishes but I hadn't. I gave mine to Anne Greenwood.
From Steven

Dear Steven,
Thank you for the pen and writing pad. I am using them now. You left your jumper here. I will bring it to school on Monday, And you spelt sandwitches wrong.
From Shirley

THE CINEMA. 1979 Age 19
Steve,
We are going to the pictures to see The Life of Brian at 7.00 o'clock. Do you want to come? Anne and Tony are going, too. I'll post this through your letter-box so I hope your dog doesn't eat it.
Shirley

Dear Shirley,
Nothing else on so OK. Meet you outside at quarter to 7. I hope your cat doesn't eat this.

Shirley,
I waited and waited and only Anne turned up. So we missed the start and went to that new retro milk bar instead. They have those pyrex cups that tip up when you pick them up and my coffee went all over Anne's skirt so we had to go to her house so she could change. So one way and another it was all a bit of a disaster. And her mum had gone to visit her sister, so I tried to get the stains out for her, not very successfully.
Steve

Steven,
Oh, sorry. I wasn't feeling very well. Tony knew because he came to meet me at our house. He was supposed to go and tell you. Anne has just been round and she told me all about what happened last night, about her mum and dad being out when you got to their house. And what you did. She says she didn't think it was an accident, you spilling the coffee. And it has ruined her skirt. Amongst other things.
Shirley

Shirl,
She's a liar. I didn't do anything.

THE WEDDING 1980 Age 19
Dear Shirley,
You asked what we would like for a wedding present. We'll be living at her mum's for a while so we don't need much, only Anne said one of those fluffy bedspreads would be nice for these winter nights. It could be a combined wedding and Christmas present. There is a stall in the market sells them. They have got some half price. Anne says an orange one, please, if possible. And, in answer to your question, no, Tony Brown has not been invited to the wedding.
Steve

Dear Steve,
I am really sorry to hear that Anne is poorly. And so soon after your wedding. Has she eaten something that has upset her? Tony seemed quite upset when I told him. He is thinking of applying for a transfer and moving elsewhere. Anyway, give her my love and let me know if there is anything I can do.
Shirley

THE BABY 1980 Age 19
Shirl, Great news but a bit of a shock. I'm going to be a dad. I hope I can cope. I'm still a kid myself. But Ann's mother says she will look

after it while we are both at work. Steve

Dear Steve and Anne,
Congratulations! I can't wait to see little Tracey. What weight is she? I was going to knit a matinee jacket but as the baby has come so early I will buy a tiny one and a little hat to match that should fit a premature baby. I'll come on the bus to see you all on Saturday, if that's all right. P.S. Sorry about the card. The corner shop only had cards for baby boys.
Love Shirley xxx

Dear Shirley.
Ann says please buy a larger size as the baby will grow into it if it s too big now, Actually, she is quite a plump little thing,
Love. Steve and Ann.

MEETING AGAIN. 1988 Age 28
Dear Shirley,
Thanks for the invitation to visit you in your new abode. Anne says she'd love to come but is going to see her mother who is not very well. Tracey is going to have a sleep-over at a friend's house. But I'll be free that weekend, so, if you don*t mind, I'll look you up and drop in for a coffee. How's the job? We are all missing you.
Love, Steve and Anne

Dear Steve,
It was lovely to see you again and catch up on all your news. Thanks for the bottle of wine. You left your scarf here. You always were forgetful. Please collect it sometime soon or I shall wear it. Give my love to Anne and Tracey.
Shirley x

Shirl, I'll come for the scarf on Saturday. Anne will be visiting her mother again so she won't be able to come. Remember, I don't eat

eggs. Wrap up warm. It forecasts snow.
Love, Steve

TONY BROWN 1998 Age 38
Dear Steve,
Guess what. I went to Wolverhampton to do some shopping and guess who I bumped into. Tony Brown, looking very affluent. He's got some managerial job somewhere. He did say where but I've forgotten. He asked after you and Anne and Tracey so I told him your new address. I hope I did the right thing as I know you are not keen on him. He said he might call round to see you all sometime.
Love to you all,
Shirley

Dear Shirley,
You were right when you said I wasn't keen on Tony Brown. Yesterday afternoon I finished early so I caught an earlier bus home from work just in time to catch sight of Tony Brown driving off in a hurry. Anne was all flustered and she said she had a headache and went to bed. Tracey did her homework and then went to see her friend, so I went down the pub and called at the chippy on my way back, by which time Tracey was in the bathroom and Anne was fast asleep. So I don't know what Tony Brown said to upset her, but he'd better watch out if he knocks on our door again when I'm not there.
Steven

Sorry, Steve.
My fault, sorry, sorry, really sorry.
Shirley

SHIRLEY'S 44th BIRTHDAY. 2004 Age 44
Dear Ann and Steve,
Sorry I haven't written for ages. Time is flying too quickly. I'll be celebrating my 44th birthday on Saturday. Do you remember my

14th? 30 years ago. Where did the time go? Would you all like to come for a meal? I promise no eggs. It would be great to see you after so long and recapture our youth.
Love, Shirley

Hi Shirl,
Yes, same here, 44. It doesn't seem five minutes since we were 14. Of course I remember your 14th birthday party! Who could forget that? Ann will be on a weekend course, and Tracey has left home now she's finished at uni, but I'd love to come for a free meal instead of opening a tin of beans. I'll bring a bottle.

Steve, that's fine, but you'll have to wash up. Sorry Anne can't come, though.

A FEW DAYS LATER 2004 Age 44
It was great seeing you again, Shirl. Here's to the next time.

Steve, there won't be a next time. Not if you behave like that again.

THE REVELATION 2006 Age 46
Shirley's phone rings.
Hello.

Shirley, is that you? It's me, Steven.

Steven? Steven Hudson? That's odd. I was thinking of you only this morning and suddenly you ring out of the blue. The last time I saw you it was my birthday, remember? Why are you phoning? I told you not to phone. Is everything all right? How's Anne? How's Tracey? Is anything wrong?

Shirley, I need to talk to you. I have a problem. I'm feeling really depressed. Things are not too good between me and Anne, one way and another. Anne had sort of shut herself off. I thought she was ill or something and wasn't telling me. But I have found out she has been seeing that bastard Tony Brown on a regular basis. Turns out they have been meeting up for years, mostly at his place, when she said she was on a weekend course or visiting her mother or some other excuse. I don't know what is going to happen, but I can't go on like this.

Oh hell, Steve, that's awful. Tony Brown always was a creep. What about Tracey? Does she know what has been going on?

Tracey is a librarian in Reading. She has a flat there. We don't see her very often, Christmas and such.

Steve, I'm really, really sorry. I don't know what I can do to help but I'm here if you need me. Keep in touch. Take care, Steve

THE BREAKUP 2009 Age 49
Shirley's phone rings.

Shirley? It's Steve. It's all over.

Steve? What is all over?

Me and Anne. We tried to patch it up but it wasn't working. She said she had given up seeing that bastard but she's been seen out with him holding hands, two or three times recently, at that restaurant that everyone raves about out in one of the villages, so one of my mates said. Thought I should know, he said. We had a big bust up last night. I said to Anne that I didn't know how Tracey would react when she heard about her and Brown. Anne said, 'Oh she knows. She's known for years.' Tracey had questioned our wedding date and her date of birth and asked her mother if we'd had it off before the wedding. But, you know, we hadn't. That's when Anne told her. She begged her not to tell me that she knew. That bastard's her dad. I could have killed him. And her. We had a huge row, shouting accusations, screaming, crying. When I came home tonight Anne had gone. Wardrobe empty. Left a note on the table that she was moving in with him. So that's it, Shirl. I'll file for a divorce and be free of her. I could do without this at my age. I need a lot of TLC.

I'm here, Steve. Come.

THE KISS 2012 Age 52
Shirley, it's all sealed and finished. The decree absolute came today. I called in at the estate agent's and put the house on the market. I can't bear to live here anymore. I'll have to give her half, but it should fetch a good price. I can apply for a transfer from work to a branch near you. so I should be able to pay my way and have a good bit in the bank as well. So, how about it, Shirley, my love? Shall we fix a date?

If that's a proposal, Steve, I'm ready and waiting. In fact, I have been ready and waiting since that time you kissed me at my 14th birthday party. Do you remember when we played Forfeits, years ago, when I was 14? I've been in love all this time. Then you married Anne. And I have ached for you ever since.

Yes, I remember that kiss. I was so embarrassed with everyone watching.

You said 'urgh" and wiped your mouth with the back of your hand. I thought you hated it.

Course not. Come here, then, Shirley, my love, and I'll give you a proper one. Close your eyes. Here it comes.

And they kiss. A nervous little peck at first, then one that becomes tender and loving. **Wendy Goulstone**

February 16

Wedding Vows

Diana made her way along the row and sat primly on the bench, feeling a shiver of excitement run through her as she looked at the catwalk in front. She was so looking forward to helping Beatrice plan her dream wedding, and especially with choosing her wedding gown. She had always vowed that any daughter of hers would have the best money could buy; nothing like the shabby wedding she'd had to suffer because of her mother's penny pinching ways.

She couldn't understand why Beatrice had insisted her gran come along. They had always been close, she thought resentfully, but really! Wedding dress shopping should be a mother and daughter experience. They were here now though, so she supposed she might as well make the best of it. She just hoped her mother behaved herself.

She was jolted out of her daydream as Mavis flopped down next to her, dumping a heavy handbag between them.

'Gawd save us. I'm jiggered!'

'Mother! Be careful. This jacket was expensive.' Diana pulled the edges tightly together. 'And put your bag on the floor,' she inched uncomfortably to the edge of the seat, 'other people want to sit down.'

'I'm keeping a seat for Bea,' Mavis harrumphed, 'and anyway, I ain't putting me bag on the floor. Someone might nick it.'

'Well, put it somewhere,' Diana clipped, 'Beatrice is here now.'

Mavis hoisted her bag onto her lap and hefted her bulk to the right, clumsily sticking an elbow into the side of the woman next to her.

'They don't give a body much room here do they!' she huffed as Beatrice eased into the seat vacated by the bag, carrying three bubbling flute glasses. 'What's that? Ain't they got no tea? I could murder a cuppa.'

Diana pressed her lips tightly together, her rigid fingers picking and flicking unconsciously at her nails. It was going to be a long day.

Beatrice put her arm around her gran's shoulder, 'Are you OK?'

''Course I am. Just not used to all this palaver is all. I never had no white dress when I married your grandad. I wore a lovely blue costume I'd made meself, and I had white gloves and a navy handbag.' Her eyes glazed over at the memory. 'Lasted me for years that costume did before I cut it down for your mother. Remember the skirt and jacket I made for you Di?'

Diana felt her shoulders tighten; she remembered it very well. While the other girls turned up for their college interviews in trendy miniskirts or bell bottoms, she wore that awful knee length skirt and matching jacket her mother made from her old wedding suit. The enduring nickname Dowdy Di had followed her right through college, until she got her first job and was able to afford a tiny bedsit and finally dress in the latest high street fashions. Flexing her aching fingers she took a gulp from her glass.

'You look gorgeous in your wedding photo, Gran.'

'Thanks darling and so will you. Just watch your pennies; you'll need your money later on when the babbies come. And don't listen to your mother,' she added in a stage whisper, 'she always did have ideas above her station.' She raised her glass and took a drink. 'Ooh! The bubbles went right up me nose. This is quite nice, ain't it.'

+ +

Mavis clutched her bag tightly to her chest and sat up straight as the music started and the first model stepped onto the catwalk. She loved clothes and had always been a whizz with the sewing machine, managing to turn tatty old cast-offs into something of quality. Her Di had been one of the best dressed kids on their street; no cheap looking high street fashions for her, not when Mavis could make proper clothes. She tilted her chin proudly at the memories.

The model strutted down the catwalk and as she towered haughtily in front of them Mavis pointed an accusing finger.

'Good Gawd! That dress ain't even finished.'

'Mother, be quiet.'

'But you can see the boning in the corset,' Mavis persisted, 'and her skin underneath. It's indecent!'

'It's the fashion, Gran, although not one I would choose,' Beatrice whispered.

'Thank Gawd for that. You couldn't walk into church in that state.'

'For the hundredth time, Mother,' Diana snarled through clenched teeth, 'she's not... getting... married... in... a... church.'

But Mavis was heedlessly nudging Beatrice's arm. 'Cor! I like that, classic white satin with a bit of a sleeve. Reminds me of yours, don't ya reckon, Di?'

Diana winced at the memory of her wedding dress which her mother had made from satin bought at the local market. She had been bitterly indifferent to any compliments; forever resentful that they couldn't afford the exquisite lace Pronuptia dress she had set her heart on.

'That were a cracker of a day, weren't it, Di! I hope Bea's knees up is as good.' Mavis chortled at the memories.

'Beatrice's day will be nothing like mine. She certainly won't have to run the gauntlet of drunken men and jutting snooker cues to get to a reception in the back room of a working men's club,' Diana asserted.

'We were lucky to get that room for free,' Mavis prickled. 'Mind you they took more money off your father there than we ever did, so I reckon we deserved it.'

Diana flinched, then straightening her back, pointed to the model sashaying down the catwalk in a pearl encrusted white sheath dress. In a quivering voice she said, 'Beatrice, look at that, it's beautiful.'

'That's so tight she can hardly walk,' Mavis interrupted loudly. 'Imagine trying to go for a wee in that!'

'Trust you to lower the tone,' Diana hissed, ignoring the shaking shoulders of the women in front.

'Sor-ry! I'm just being practical is all,' Mavis grumbled. 'I reckon I could make you a cracking dress for a fraction of the cost, Bea.'

Leaning slightly forward she flung, 'I've got some lovely old netting somewhere,' at Diana's bowed head before announcing, 'Ere! Look at those blokes. Your grandad used to wear a cap like that for work.'

'They're modelling suits for the groom, Gran. It's a *Peaky Blinders* thing; all the fashion now.'

'It's a blinder all right. As bad as he was, your grandad wouldn't be seen out in his work clothes.'

Diana rose majestically amidst a burst of sniggers. 'I don't feel well. I'm going home.' Head down, she excused her way through the crowd, quickly followed by Beatrice and a blundering Mavis.

'Mum! Please stay. I want to try some dresses on. That's why we're here.'

'I've got some paracetamol in me bag,' Mavis offered helpfully.

Diana turned towards them, patted her eyes with a tissue and snapped a curt, 'It's fine. I'm fine. I just need a few moments on my own. I'll see you in the café in a while,' before making her way to the exit.

+ +

Beatrice put the tray on the table, 'Here's your tea, Gran. I got us a sandwich too. We'll get Mum something when she comes back.'

'I don't know what's up with her, Bea. She don't get her snooty ways from me and certainly not from her dad.'

'I think she just wants everything to be perfect for me. I don't think she enjoyed her wedding; I've never even seen a picture. She says she hasn't got any and Dad just says to leave him out of it.'

Mavis pulled an old envelope out of her bag. 'Good job I've got one then. Don't tell her though. Lucky I was there when she went on her rampage and I managed to salvage this before she burnt it with the others.'

'Oh Gran! Her dress was beautiful. Did you really make it? And I love the long veil.'

'Yes. I made it. And despite what your mum might say that veil was shop bought. She saved for ages, did overtime too when she could. It looked lovely floating behind her walking down the aisle.'

Mavis cast a worried look at Beatrice, 'You will be walking down the aisle won't you, Bea? All this nonsense from your mum about you not getting married in church...'

'We're getting married in a barn, Gran. It's part of a big country house estate and it's beautiful. You'll love it, honest you will.'

'A barn eh! OK, Bea, I'll take your word for it, but won't it be a bit mucky? You might want to get a short dress.'

'No, Gran. I promise you it will be perfectly clean. Look, here's Mum.'

Diana pulled up a chair and sat down stiffly.

'You OK, Di? Want a sandwich?'

'No, thank you, Mother, I'm fine'

'Mum, I didn't know you had a veil when you got married. I want a long one too.'

Mavis threw a worried glance at Beatrice who responded with a quick shake of her head and a smile.

'I'd forgotten actually. I had a beautiful long veil from Pronuptia. It was all delicate lace and flowers. Who told you?'

'I did, Di. We was just talking.'

'But when I was walking into the reception one of those big oafs stood on it and ripped it.'

'I think that was your dad, Di.'

'It most certainly wasn't. It was one of those ruffians in the club.'

'Nope, it were your dad...'

'Mum! Gran! Please don't start again. Lets go and have a look at the dresses shall we? Are you OK with that Mum?'

'I'll be fine. Let's just get this done. Lead on, Beatrice.'

+ +

Two hours later a radiant Beatrice emerged from behind a curtain in a froth of lace. 'This is the one! I can't believe I've found the dress of my dreams.'

Gazing tearfully at her daughter standing there looking beautiful in the very dress that she would have chosen for herself, Diana smiled. 'Matthew is a very lucky man, Beatrice, you look exquisite.'

Beatrice spun around. 'I'm going to feel like I'm floating down the aisle.'

Mavis looked at her granddaughter and wiped a tear from her eye. 'They don't have aisles in barns, Bea. You'll be walking down the middle.'

'But it will feel like an aisle to me, Gran.'

'Well, that's lovely, Bea but I just think it's a bit weird is all.'

'It's the latest fashion, Mother. Everyone's doing it.'

'That's all right then,' Mavis challenged, 'Perish the thought you wouldn't be in with the crowd, Di.'

'Gran you'll love it, I promise.' Beatrice squeezed her gran's hand, 'This dress is perfect, and right within my budget.'

'What budget? I'm not letting me only granddaughter buy her own wedding dress. I had to scrimp and scrape for your mum's but I'm doing all right now and I can afford it, so I'm paying.' She turned to Diana who was staring incredulously at her. 'Oh I know you were disappointed with your wedding, Di, and I vowed I would make it up to you one day.' She took Diana's hand. 'But it ain't been easy and this is the first chance I've had, so...'

Her eyes dropped, 'I thought Bea said you was getting your nails done yesterday, Di.'

Diana looked at her nails which had been so perfectly manicured when she left home that morning. Now, after hours of involuntary picking, slivers of red polish were missing and some were stuck to her black wool skirt.

'Never mind, Di,' Mavis put her arm through her daughter's, pinching her none too gently in the process. 'Once we've organised the dress, we'll go and find somewhere to get your nails sorted, my treat. And I want to go and look for some posh boots or wellies. I don't care what you say, a barn's a barn and I ain't chancing stepping in anything in good shoes.'

Rosemary Marks

February 17

Big Spender

The car park of the Mason's Arms was full, vehicles crammed into every available space. Debbie was worried she would be late if she had to go and park in a side street. Then, just as she had started to reverse out, she spotted a gap at the back by the fence, where weeds were bursting out through the chain-links and attacking the tarmac. It was a tight squeeze between a rusty, white Ford Fiesta and a newish maroon Vauxhall, but she made it. Opening the door carefully, she wriggled out, then leaned back in for her bulky holdall. She shimmied her way between the two cars, holding the bag above her head.

With the car park that full, the pub had to be busy. She liked a good crowd, the tips were better. Turning up her coat collar and hunching her shoulders, she shoved open the heavy door and entered the saloon bar. The usual sounds and smells washed over her: loud voices discussing soaps and football, raucous laughter and thumping music mingled with beer and body odour. Her attempt to avoid recognition didn't work. A couple of blokes nudged each other and leered at her.

'Over here, Blondie. I can show you a good time.'

They laughed raucously at their wit and slapped each other on the back. Debbie hurried past, ignoring them. She'd heard worse, much worse. Punters shouted out cruel and disgusting things. A stripper was just an object to them - bought and paid for. At first she'd found it humiliating to hear such vile words yelled at her and she often went home in tears. She was wiser now - she didn't listen anymore - and she never looked them in the eye.

The barmaid was an old friend and waved her over. Debbie pushed her way through the crowd to the bar. Lisa had changed her hair again. This week it was red and piled up high. Debbie didn't think the colour or the style suited her, but she wasn't going to say so. At least Lisa wasn't wearing the white frilly blouse that made her look like a sad middle-aged tart. She always dressed so badly and wore far too much make-up. Debbie had often wanted to drop the odd hint, but Lisa would only take it personally.

'Upstairs,' Lisa said and jerked her thumb at the ceiling.

Debbie nodded and went through the door at the end of the bar that led to the loos and the stairs to the function room. She took off her coat and hung it over the bannisters, shaking out long, blonde hair. It hung almost to her waist. Underneath the wig her short mousy crop was plastered to her scalp, making it sweaty and itchy. She stepped into the Ladies, turning her nose up at the familiar aroma of urine, bleach and stale perfume.

It smelt as though the flush had stopped working again. Debbie pushed open the cubicle door, wondering for the millionth time why there was only one toilet provided for the pub's female patrons and why it had to be so disgusting. As usual, there was no loo paper, unless she counted the stuff littering the floor, and she didn't. She'd sooner pee in the car park. It had to be part of the male conspiracy to keep women out of pubs, unless they were behind the bar or taking their clothes off. There was no soap and only the cold tap worked, providing a small trickle of water. Debbie hoped there was somewhere else for staff to wash their hands. She never ate or drank anything here, and this place was one of the better ones.

Balancing first on one leg and then on the other, she swapped her trainers for high-heeled thigh-length boots that zipped up at the back for easy removal. Mouth wide open, she added more black mascara to her false eyelashes and then applied lip-liner and layers of bright red lipstick. She pulled on long, black evening gloves and draped a feather boa around her neck. Her music was ready, volume turned up high. She blew herself a kiss in the mirror. It was cracked, but at least it worked, unlike the toilet.

The door swung shut behind her, cutting off the smell of disinfectant. Debbie climbed the stairs carefully, wary of her spike heels, bag slung over one shoulder, holding the bannister in one hand. At the top she stopped and put the holdall down.

+   +

Moira Baker looked at her guests, an assorted bunch of friends, colleagues and family, with nothing in common except Gerry. She wished she'd been able to afford something better for him than this pub, but now that his salary had stopped, there wasn't much spare cash to waste. The landlord had done his best on her limited budget and the room was clean. The buffet was laid out on an old trestle table, but she had brought the white damask table cloth from home. It had been a wedding present from her Auntie Ivy, and she only used it on special occasions. This was one. Washed and starched, it hung in stiff folds, looking like new.

There was plenty of food: cold meat and salads, sausage rolls, quiches, cheese and French bread. Beer and wine bottles were lined up next to paper plates, but at least the cutlery wrapped in paper napkins was not plastic and neither were the glasses.

Chairs lined the walls, but nobody seemed inclined to sit. They stood about in groups, chatting quietly: Gerry's sister Anne, her husband Tom and their two teenage sons; Moira's sister Lesley and her three daughters; Alan Harrison and Karen Brown from Gerry's office; their next-door neighbours, Monica and Sam; and, of course, their own children, Mark and Linda. They stood by her, hovering protectively. They were good kids and she was proud of them.

More guests were coming up the stairs. Auntie Ivy wheezed like a steam train as she finally reached the top. Moira was delighted to see how many of Gerry's friends and colleagues had turned out. Everyone had a drink and she wondered if she should make a little speech, thank them all for coming and propose a toast to Gerry.

+   +

On the landing Debbie took a deep breath, turned on the music and pushed open the door of the function room. As the trumpets blared out and Shirley Bassey started singing Big Spender, Debbie strutted into the room with a bump and a grind, long blonde hair tossed back.

Thirty smartly dressed people were standing in small groups and quietly chatting. As Debbie entered, conversations halted in mid-sentence and the room froze as if someone had pressed pause. She slowly peeled off one shoulder length black glove, a finger gripped between her teeth. At first she didn't notice their appalled faces, she never made eye contact with the punters, but the lack of response and the strange silence made her look at them. The black ties, the women's sombre dark suits and the outraged expressions told her that these people had not gathered for Jimmy Peacock's stag night.

The black feather boa slid from her shoulders, *Big Spender* still booming out. Debbie saw the mourners' horrified faces, their mouths wide open in shock. Slowly she backed away. What could she possibly say? She reached the door and bent down to switch off the music. Shirley Bassey was abruptly cut off.

'I'm so terribly sorry,' she said. 'I must have come to the wrong pub. I'm really, really sorry.'

The feather boa lay crumpled in the middle of the floor like a dead crow. The room was still completely silent. Debbie didn't wait for a reply. She stumbled back downstairs as fast as the spike heels would allow, grabbing her coat at the foot of the stairs and quickly slipping it on to hide her black basque and stockings.

Lisa was waiting for her in the bar, a gloating smile on her face, a big bloated spider in the middle of her web.

'Didn't take you long,' she said. 'Didn't they like you? You being such hot stuff with your wonderful, sexy body?' She almost spat the last words at Debbie.

Debbie stared at Lisa in astonishment. What was she on about? Lisa had always had a spiteful streak, but Debbie hadn't realised that she'd upset her. What had she done to deserve this? Whatever it was, Lisa must have been brooding over it for weeks, planning her revenge as her resentment festered, waiting for the right moment. She didn't even care that she would be poisoning a long friendship over some imagined slight.

Debbie leant over the bar and hissed at Lisa, 'That was a really nasty thing to do.'

Lisa studied her French manicure. The nails were false; they were too long to be real.

'Was it?' she said in an overly sweet voice. 'I thought it was rather funny.'

'It's not about me. What about those people upstairs? What have they ever done to you?'

Lisa pouted, her eyes shifting away from Debbie.

'Nothing,' she mumbled.

'Imagine how you'd feel,' Debbie continued, her voice hoarse with anger. 'You've just buried someone you love, maybe your grandma.'

Lisa flinched.

'And some stupid, spiteful cow sends a stripper to the wake. Don't you ever think about other people, about how they might feel? Or do you only think about yourself?'

A stubborn expression crossed Lisa's face.

'And I thought we were friends, best mates, you always said. Who does that to her best mate?'

Lisa shrugged and said nothing. Debbie could see that Lisa wasn't prepared to give an inch. There was no point in talking to her any longer. Debbie could tell the landlord what Lisa had done, but that would achieve nothing. Lisa would only hate her even more. Even when they were kids, Lisa had harboured grudges, but Debbie had never thought she would be on the receiving end. They were friends, weren't they? Not any more.

Debbie picked up her bag and turned to go. Standing in front of her was one of the mourners, a woman dressed in a black wool suit that had seen better days. She was holding Debbie's feather boa.

'I am so sorry. I can't apologise enough. I don't know how the mix-up happened. I must have written it down wrong.'

'Don't apologise, my dear. You and I both know exactly what happened. You were the victim of a nasty, so-called prank.'

Lisa, who had been listening eagerly, hoping to hear the widow tear a strip off Debbie, suddenly moved to the other end of the bar to serve a thirsty customer who had been waiting impatiently for her to notice him.

Debbie saw that the woman wasn't upset or angry with her. Although her eyes were sad, there was a hint that a keen sense of humour was hidden within.

'And,' Moira continued, 'I think that my husband would have been highly amused by a stripper at his funeral. Why don't you come back upstairs with me and have a drink in Gerry's memory?'

She draped the feather boa round Debbie's neck.

'Don't bother getting changed. You are wearing black.'

Fran Neatherway

February 18

A Good Story, But I Don't Believe A Word Of It

(Read to the soundtrack of Bluegrass music)
We landed at O'Hare and rented an SUV. We enjoyed driving across the Midwest from Chicago to Kansas City and one of the things we liked most was to listen to 181FM on the satellite radio. As you know, that's that great Bluegrass channel - Front Porch Radio.

We always drove with our elbows resting on the open window, because that way, we felt authentic.

Our overnight stop was to be in Unionville, Iowa, but we were getting hungry, so we started looking for a diner.

Suddenly the music stopped and the news came on. There had been a tragedy in Canada. A young man had been killed when a maple tree exploded. His brother was being interviewed. He explained that back when the First Nation peoples managed the maple forests, they regularly tapped off the maple syrup. But now they had left the forests, and the white man didn't know he had to drain the trees. Every now and then the syrup would ferment inside one of the trees and the pressure would make the tree explode - violently and unpredictably.

The poor young man had been hiking with friends when it happened. He never knew what hit him. His brother was distraught, and complained that warning signs should be put up along the hiking trails. We were shocked; we had never imagined this could happen.

Then we came across The Donut Diner.

The lady who served us was the owner. Maybe she didn't get many foreigners in; she was very chatty and asked us questions about our journey. Eventually the conversation turned to the dreadful story on the Front Porch Radio news.

She listened to us, then she looked at the calendar on the wall, then she looked back at us. 'It's a good story, but I don't believe a word of it. Have you seen the date?'

Philip Gregge

February 19

Togetherness

Brenda Parkinson pushed her shopping trolley toward the post office.

"*Cthulhu lives!!*" was sprayed in green on the Western Union poster.

"That's new," she mumbled to herself.

The HR gang watched her like a pride of lions. Sandy thought HR always stood for Human Remains, not realising it was his mum's favourite mis-acronym.

"Get the chloroform, this is the last one," hissed Sandy. "We are finally leaving this dump tonight."

Unwisely Brenda stopped in the doorway of the derelict Peacocks store, and they had her, but not before she kicked Sandy in the groin and knocked one of Morgan's teeth out.

"Get stronger stuff next time," shouted Kev out of Brenda's range.

Waking up in the disused community centre, Brenda saw the others; three older men and a younger slim woman in her thirties, bound tightly with motorbike locks. Daemon signatures on each in cardboard looking like Croatian beermats.

"I like the doily patterns you drawn on 'em lads." She wasn't taking this very seriously at all.

Sandy threatened her. "We are after your bloody soul you silly cow."

"Eighteen years' factory work destroyed mine, dear, ha, ha."

The other captives were laughing strangely because their mouths were full of shredded Brexit leaflets. But Big Steve would not take his medicine.

"Eat your words, Brexiteer. We prepared it nicely for you," menaced Doug Less

Morgan had to force feed him the bits of Farage's picture but he spat them straight out.

"Pin 'em on 'im."

"What?"

"The Brexit bits!" said Sandy.

Almost ready but Morgan seemed worried. "Won't Lord of Darkness feast on us too?"

"Not with this circle of salt, Morgan, we're totally safe and the demons have to obey us. It's the first good thing to happen in six years, me discovering the Khunrath Bible."

And then came the incantation.

"I only have to acknowledge the dark realm to open it." Sandy held the occult grimoire.

HR were baffled.

He drew himself up to his full height

"Jubiläum!"

"Diese Ekstase umfasst das Reich des Todes – die Unterwelt, die Tiefe der Erde selbst, das Chthonische, Trauer und Lobpreis – wie sie gemeinsam in die Sinne einbrechen."

"Man you're giving me the creeps," said Nigel, who is called Harry.

"Get it over with, pencil neck" moaned Doug.

Forced to reassess her reality, Morgan stood in the circle rooted as an oak.

From each damned mouth or jabbed safety pin erupted squid-like tentacles in sewer green. The sacrifices writhed, pained like boiled silkworms.

Finally, a bone beak with unnaturally white teeth issued, each body blotched with sin laden green. Morgan struggled to distinguish the screams from pain-addled laughter .

The humanoid squids started to merge orgiastically into one writhing mess with ten incongruous legs that Kev thought were hilarious. If only he could tell salt from baking powder.

"No," Morgan cried. "We're all in it together!!"

Unhindered the tentacles touched them all, devouring, corrupting and eventually putrefying the hosts. All but one.

+ +

Later. Brenda Parkinson pushed her shopping trolley toward the pub. On a black board, PENSIONERS SERVED EVERY DAY!!

"Delicious." She grinned.

Chris Wright

February 20

Temptation

The roar of the engine made it clear that something unusual was coming round the corner of St John's Wood Road. Beth stood on the pavement, a little anxious and not too close to the traffic. She had arranged to meet Jez for an afternoon out. Their initial chat in the garden of a city pub had been pleasant and engaging. She was impressed with his geniality, his self-deprecating humour and the unsaid air of mystery about him.

Jez ran his own design company, which was clearly going well. His clothes were finely-cut, his sunglasses out of the top drawer, and his shoes - she noticed - were impeccable. But what was he like as a person?

"Shall we meet at two?" he asked. "I'll pick you up in my motor."

Not much to go on there; it seemed a reasonable arrangement, but she had picked up a slight smirk in his manner as he mentioned the word 'motor', almost old-fashioned in its usage, as if driving around London might be a pleasure rather than a trial. What could he mean?

When the Ferrari appeared, nearly every head turned. The drinkers outside the Duke of York stopped their conversations as Jez indicated and pulled to a stop next to Beth. A couple of revellers came out of the pub to see what the fuss was all about.

Beth was a little embarrassed. She wasn't keen on being the centre of attention, especially when it was foisted on her by another. The passenger window lowered automatically. Jez leaned across and said - somewhat unbelievably, "Take a seat, babe." Was this irony? Did he really talk like that when he was behind the wheel? When she looked inside, his left arm was hooked around the passenger seat as if a partial embrace was almost compulsory.

Instinctively, she drew back. Is this where she wanted her life to go - a subordinate player to both Jez the high-flyer and his motorised plaything? Was she just another trophy for Jez to display?

Despite the flashy motor, Beth was not impressed. In fact she was repulsed, driven back by her own emotions.

"Sorry, Jez. I tried to call you. I've been called into work urgently. They can't do without me this afternoon," she lied.

Jez didn't know what to say, except to allow his foot to play on the accelerator. Left all alone to fiddle with his gearstick, he pulled away into the flow of traffic.

John Howes

February 21

Carrots

Sunday 6th March
Dear Diary,
We've just finished lunch and I'm writing this now so I don't forget.

Dad was harping on about eating our vegetables again. I get that they're full of goodness and all that, but they just don't taste great. Peas taste of nothing, and carrots overpower everything else on your plate with their weird juiciness. You can't even try to hide them in your mash or with your beef. When you've got even a speck of that evil orange on your fork, all you can taste is carrot.

'If you don't eat everything on your plate, you're not getting pudding,' Dad said, as he always does.

But Mom had given me the chopped up equivalent of about six carrots. I couldn't eat them all. It was far too much for anyone to consume. I had concerns about turning orange.

So I left a few.

'Are you going to eat all your carrots up?' Dad said, with that warning tone to his voice. 'Your sister and brother managed to eat everything.'

Without even thinking about it, some words came pummelling out of my mouth.

'They're my lucky carrots,' I said.

'Lucky carrots?' my dad asked, incredulously.

'Yeah. I read somewhere that it was good luck to leave two or three carrots at the end of a meal. It's worth a shot to see if it brings me luck.'

I said this with such conviction that even I started to believe it.

No one knew what to say. There was this bizarre silence around the table, where everyone was clearly trying to work out whether I was serious or not. I held my face straight.

I was waiting for the laughter. I was prepared for the ridicule. I was expecting to eat these now cold bits of carrot or forfeit my dessert.

But nothing happened.

'Okay,' my dad said. 'Who's going to help me whip the cream?'

That was it. They all bought it. Weirdest few moments of my life.

So, from now on, I always have to leave two or three carrots at the end of every Sunday lunch. I must see this through. Leaving carrots is lucky and I strongly believe this.

Please don't forget this. This is the new you.

I'll report back next week,

Lindsay Woodward

February 22

My Lucky Number

For those of you who remember 1967 and the tv series *The Prisoner*, or for those who have worked in many industries, you will sympathise with the sentiment: "I am not a number, I am a free man."

Eight years later, in October 1975, I left my first career in the transport industry (as a lorry driver) after my first born said to his mother, "There's a man in the kitchen," and went into warehousing and logistics (a warehouseman) so I could see my children grow up and recognise me.

I was allocated the two little ducks number twenty-two as my employee number. I thought this job would last for a couple of years and I would move on. Every bit of paperwork even including my wage slip identified me as twenty-two. My colleagues, of course, had other names we called each other, sometimes not very complimentary but not many with any malice intended. After some differences of opinion in the early days between the company, the workers and me as their representative, we ended up with market-leading wages and conditions making our positions the proverbial golden handcuffs so as number twenty-two I was not unlike *The Prisoner* working in what seemed an ideal environment. Some thirty-two years later when I retired; what turned out to be my lucky number twenty-two had paid for my young family growing up and paid off my mortgage.

As I never tried to escape, I was never aware of any giant balloons pursuing me on the Rugby Road home.

Patrick Garrett

February 23

Lovebite

It was 1960 and I was fifteen-ish. My friend Anne Henderson had moved from Sutton Coldfield to Betws-y-Coed in the wilds of Wales. Her father had been a bus driver, changed career and had become a gamekeeper on an estate in Betws-y-Coed. I was to stay with her for a week before joining the rest of our family on the Llynn. We used to hire a farmhouse for our two families and we did some amazing holidays over the years there. I think my Uncle Kelvin must have driven me there.

Anyway, I had a lovely week there with her and her family in very different surroundings. On our last night, we got all dressed up and walked down to the main road. Anne said it was quite safe; she did it often. So we thumbed a lift into Llanrwst, the nearby town. A pop lorry stopped for us. We had a wander round the town and then two lads joined us out of a pub. They must have been about 19.

They had a grey Mini van. I was to sit in the back with Dai and Anne in the front with the driver. They had both some beer partaken.

Dai was talking to me romantically in Welsh. I got the gist so I said I do not understand but the answer is no no no. I had to hold his hands so I could know where they were. I did let him kiss me and that was nice. Anne had a curfew so eventually we were home and safe and crept up to bed.

The next morning Anne was having a fit. It seems I had a lovebite on my neck. I didn't even know what it was. She used her makeup to disguise it because she said if her mother saw it, she wouldn't be allowed out again. We live and learn don't we?

Then Uncle came and got me and we went to have our family visit at Abersoch.

Ruth Hughes

February 24

Homecoming

Yes, I'm down on my luck. I've done a lot of things I shouldn't do, and spent too much money doing them. I'm hoping for a job. Any job. The last job I had was looking after some pigs, and the pigs were better fed than I was.

I don't expect much from my father, after the way I behaved. But at least I hope to have somewhere to sleep, something to eat and a lot of hard work.

What will I say to my mother? She always wanted a grandchild. How do I tell her she probably has a grandchild but I don't know where or who?

Then there's Jake, my brother. Our relationship was always… awkward, especially when I left. Perhaps he'll be put in charge of me. That would be difficult, but hey, it's a living.

Round the hill, there's the farm, and there's my father. Well, he seems pleased to see me. At least that's something.

Jim Hicks

February 25

Return To The Crematorium

She walked round the crematorium garden, hoping for a sign of emerging spring bulbs pushing through the cold earth. It all looked so different today. The bare branches of the deciduous trees were stark against the pale grey sky, the tall pines were darkly imposing at the side of the memorial garden, and the evergreen shrubs were either a bright acid green, or a glaucous blue-grey. Frost-shrivelled funeral flowers, laid out at the back of the building, formed a stream of muted colours across the fancy block paving.

Last July it had been so different. The place had been bursting with colour from the underplanting, the shrubs that were tinged flame-red where the sun had touched them, the various birds flashing from cover to cover and through the tree canopy, and at the back of the crematorium the multi-coloured floral tributes had glowed in the bright sunlight, attracting bees and butterflies.

Today the garden was quiet, empty, except for her, and her thoughts of Simeon. She didn't know why she had come here today. She wrapped her coat around her, and perched on the edge of a bench. The coat was thick, woollen, fully lined, but still she felt chilled to the bone. After just a few minutes she got to her feet and resumed walking.

She had already identified the place where she had scattered Simeon's ashes at the end of August, and she didn't want to go back that way, so she slowly walked through the gloomy carpark. There were a few more cars there now, with people sitting in them. She had almost reached the far side when, as if responding to some secret signal, all the car doors opened and the people got out. They turned to look in her direction, and she thought how creepy that seemed.

There was a moment or two of silence, and then a quiet muttering began. Alarmed, she picked up her pace, and headed for the front doors of the low building. The people from the cars slowly followed. Her heart was pounding, and she was distressed to see the crematorium office was closed, as indeed were the big doors at the front.

The small crowd was right behind her now, she could hear the crunch of their steps on the gravel. She didn't need to turn and look. She didn't want to turn and look, but she didn't know what to do next, or where to go. Her car was in that car park, and not reachable.

Then a low moan broke out behind her, as three long black cars swept in through the tall wrought iron gates, and pulled up where she was standing. She stepped out of the way as the following cars started to empty, and in so doing, finally she saw the crowd that had followed her up to the building. The women were smoothing skirts and neatening their hair, the men were adjusting jackets and fiddling with shirt collars. Mourners.

From her corner she watched as the coffin was gently removed from the hearse, lifted onto a trolley, and a single cushion of white roses and lilies placed on top. Silently crying, a man and a woman took their place behind the coffin, and slowly everyone processed into the hushed room.

On impulse, she slipped in just as the doors were closing, sat apparently unremarked at the back, and read the Order of Service. A funeral for a much loved daughter, who, in despair, had taken her own life after the death of her fiancé. There, on the front of the Order of Service, Catriona saw her own name, and a photograph of her face.

Now she knew why she was there.

EE Blythe

February 26

My Short True Story

Looking back over fifty-three years, it only seems like yesterday when we were married and the first autumn of our life together was fast approaching. We were young and in many ways naive, looking forward to our lives together and all that life had in store for us. Over the space of twelve years, we had three children, all boys and the world was our oyster. Then tragedy struck and we lost our first born at the age of twelve in a road accident. Some marriages are torn apart by events like this but we clung on, even through the most terrible of times, our hopes and dreams shattered, our hearts broken, we just kept on as if in a waking nightmare to support our other two children, one only just a baby at the time.

The years past and life's season of mists and mellow fruitfulness snuck up upon us with the boys now grown up and one married, giving us two grandchildren, a girl and a boy.

We both worked hard all our lives like so many of our generation, never asking or receiving anyone's help. Paid off our mortgage after many tribulations and job changes, when finally I was made redundant and retired at the age of sixty, then worked hobby jobs till sixty five.

Now here we are and it catches me by surprise; where did the time go? It's gone so fast; once I was young and never really appreciated it, thinking I was immortal. In my youthful pride I never gave a thought that one day I would be old with my body letting me down in ways I always took for granted.

Now my beloved and I enter a new season of our lives with winter fast approaching, looking back on our time together as we both grow old, with silver hair and aching limbs. Yes, we have regrets but fate played her hand and I learned there are no what ifs, buts or maybes only the hand we were dealt.

Life, though, is not yet over, and should fate, god or whatever eternal forces there are, allow us a few more autumn's together, there are new adventures, challenges and escapades awaiting us until our leaves finally turn gold and fall making way for new life in the spring.

Patrick Garrett

February 27

1968

We were a motley crew of ragamuffin bike riders on Sundays, and after school. And all through the Summer holidays. Bicycles, of course, not one of us was able to hold a driving licence, but that didn't stop us racing around, on and off road, doing wheelies, riding two-up, and generally rejoicing in our freedom. Oh, and trying to impress the girls.

We were a mixed age bunch, mostly fourteen or fifteen, apart from Simon, who was three. Philip was the oldest, then Derek, and then me, and Toby, Arthur and Stephen were the youngest. Apart from Simon. Except, actually, Simon was older than all of us. He was very clever, and a natural leader, and we all looked up to him. But we did mercilessly tease him about his age.

The year Philip, Derek and I would turn sixteen, Simon had enjoyed his fourth birthday, and his parents had let him have a party. Sausages on sticks, pineapple cubes with cheese, different sorts of crispy things and salty crackers, and of course a big cake.

And some girls.

His parents had even left us to our own devices for part of the evening, and that's when the bottle of Strongbow got passed round, surreptitiously. We thought we were so grown up. The girls didn't.

"Well boys," boomed Mr Congreive at ten o'clock, "and ladies," he added, inclining his head towards the girls. "It's time you all went off home now." Then with a grin he produced an old paper carrier bag, and slid the empty cider bottle into it, smuggling it out to the bin under a mass of used serviettes, and waxed card trifle dishes.

Simon's parents had made a great fuss for his fourth birthday. For Simon's official fourth birthday. Of course he was sixteen, but he'd been born on the twenty ninth of February, a leap day. And as we all know, leap days only come round every fourth year. **EE Blythe**

February 28

Love In A Leap Year

I was in love with this boy called David at my school but in the boys' part. I had had a crush on him for some time, but he had no idea. I used to entwine his name with mine on all my exercise books and on my jotter. He took the same bus home as me but got off the stop before mine.

With me wanting to work in agriculture and him going to do forestry, I thought we would make a perfect match. Sometimes I got off at his stop just to see him go into his house and then I walked on to my place. It was a secret crush; he didn't know about it, only me. This was a leap year, with a 29th February, so I was going to pop the question to him on the bus home.

I worked out what I would say, that I loved him, that we should be together. I imagined him bestowing my first kiss on my lip. I had never been kissed yet. I bet he didn't have a clue. I wasn't worried about a ring; that could come later. I thought it was so romantic at fifteen or sixteen.

Cometh the hour, cometh the right day. I boarded the bus and he wasn't on it! I made my miserable way home realising I wouldn't get another chance like this for four more years. By then I was older and wiser and plenty more males had caught my eye.

Ruth Hughes

February 29

Birthdays

Charlie hated leap years, always had. Why? Because he was born on 29th February. His grandparents said that meant he was special. His other grandparents said it meant he was lucky. Charlie did not feel lucky. He felt special - but not in a good way.

It had started at primary school, when he was eight. On 29th February his teacher told the whole class that today there was a very special birthday – Charlie's - and explained why. That began the tormenting.

"You're only two, you're a baby!"

"Why aren't you at home with your mummy?"

Secondary school was no different. Word had spread of his "special" birthday and he was mocked even more. When he turned sixteen, the whole class clubbed together and gave him a cake with four candles and a card that read: **Happy Birthday now you are 4!** He had to pretend it was funny and blow out the candles, but inside he was hurt and angry. His tormentors didn't stop.

"It's only a bit of fun, leap year boy," they said.

On his eighteenth birthday, they embarrassed him in front of the whole pub by shouting, "He's too young to drink, he's only four and a half!" Everyone thought it was hilarious. Charlie was mortified by the laughter and left.

As soon as he could, Charlie moved away. If asked, he always said he was born on 1st March. He stayed at home for the next two leap year days. However, on his 28th birthday he was invited to a Leap Day party. He wanted to refuse, but it was an engagement party and unwillingly he accepted.

Lurking in a corner, he muttered, "I hate leap years."

"Me too," a voice said behind him. "It's my birthday today and I am so fed up with all the stupid comments. 'Congratulations on your seventh birthday.' Not funny the first million times."

Charlie turned round and stared into the face of a stranger. "It's my seventh birthday too," he said, and they smiled, strangers no more.

Four years later, on their eighth birthday, they married.

Fran Neatherway

If you have enjoyed
A Story for Every Day of Winter,
look out for our next anthology,
A Story for Every Day of Spring.

www.rugbycafewriters.com

Praise for our autumn anthology

'These are short stories to pick up when you have some spare time to kill, it may be on a bus or train or even sitting on a park bench soaking up the fresh air and sunshine. Give it a read.''

'Just love the concept. It's now part of my morning routine. I love the diversity of writing. Already some of these stories have stayed in my thoughts long after I have read them. Enjoyed it so much I am about to purchase their previous edition with summer stories.'

'This has a story for each day of the month for September to November. I enjoyed the variety and some of the stories were quite unexpected. It's hard to pick a favourite because they are so different. I'm looking forward to reading more from this group.'

'A lovely selection of short stories from local writers, a story a day throughout the autumn months. An easy read. Great as a gift.'

'A story for every day of autumn has a story for everyone. There's a good variety of stories and styles too. I really enjoyed this collection.'

And don't miss
Press Pause: Relax with a poem
A collection of thought-provoking poems also from the Cafe Writers of Rugby.
Available from Amazon
www.rugbycafewriters.com

About the authors

David G Bailey from East Anglia has also lived in Europe, the Caribbean, North and South America, with a base in Rugby for over forty years. His story (*A Feltwell Christmas*) in this volume is an edited extract from a third novel he published in 2023: in *Them Feltwell Boys*, parallel narratives of a schoolboy's first love affair and his career and marriage unravelling twenty-five years later converge at a school reunion. It followed *Them Roper Girls*, tracing the turbulent lives of four sisters (including the marriage of one to a Feltwell boy) from their 1950s childhood; and *Seventeen*, an adventure fantasy story aimed at and beyond young adults. To read more of and about David's work, including a quarterly newsletter and new content daily comprising extracts from diaries and other writings, visit his website www.davidgbailey.com.

EE Blythe is compelled to write. And that's all that needs to be said.

David J Boulton took up writing well into retirement from a career in the NHS, so far publishing three historical detective novels. Set in the Peak District, their protagonist has a Quaker background and the books comprise a trilogy. A fourth novel, set in the Second World War, is complete and he has embarked on a sequel. Alongside General Practice, he and his wife have run a small farm in Northamptonshire for the last thirty years. Of their two grown-up children, one lives in the Peak District with her family, their son completing a five-generation connection for the author with the area. The Writing Fiction class at the Percival Guildhouse tutored by Gill Vickery has provided the author with encouragement and inspiration, not to mention improving his grammar.

Patrick Garrett was born in a farm cottage in Perthshire, Scotland before the NHS came to be and spent the first nine years of his life on farms in Perthshire, Peeblesshire, Wigtownshire and Lanarkshire before moving to England, then two more farms in Princethorpe and Dunchurch. His father then moved to Rugby.

As Patrick is blessed with mild dyslexia, his academic career was not stellar but once he learned to read, the world became his oyster. His careers ranged from apprentice, shop assistant, removals, HGV one driver and positions in the warehouse industry. He learned to fly gliders then qualified as a CAA Microlight aircraft pilot having his flying stories published in a flying magazine. After he retired, he decided to take up local history research and write about Rugby's history. He then found Rugby Cafe Writers and says the future is yet to be written.

Wendy Goulstone has been writing for as long as she can remember. She won Stafford Children's Library playwriting competition when she was 10 years old and hasn't stopped since. This year she was joint winner of Stafford Library's Staffordshire Countryside poetry competition. Her poems have been published in *Orbis* and *The Cannon's Mouth*, and one was long-listed in the Words out Loud competition about the Covid outbreak, with a poem in the ensuing anthology, *Beyond the Storm*. She has been short-listed several times by Poetry on Loan. She is a member of several writing groups in Rugby and online, including Rugby Cafe Writers. Her furniture lies under a layer of dust and her culinary skills are basic.

Philip Gregge was an optician in Rugby for over forty years. After qualifying as an optometrist, he studied theology. As part of the leadership team of a local charismatic church, he enjoys teaching theology and has written a theology training manual for study groups. He answers theological questions in 'Let's Ask Phil', letsaskphil.org

Philip started writing Historical Fiction after waking from an anaesthetic with a plot of an Anglo-Saxon murder mystery in his head. This whetted the fascination he already had for the early Dark

Ages, and his research led him to write and publish Denua, Warrior Queen 'based on real history, but with some of history's intriguing blanks filled in'.

He is now working on a trilogy with his original murder mystery as the first part. In his spare time he plays the banjo in an Irish Music band and repairs musical instruments.

Simon Grenville is a former management trainee with the Orbit Housing Association concerned with rehousing the homeless in Milton Keynes and Central London. He is one the founding members of the Islington Community Housing Co-operative, North London, the East-West Theatre Company (Geoffrey Ost Memorial Award, University of Sheffield 1980) and the Alexandra Kollantai Film Corporation (2017). Currently trending on the Really TV Channel as Detective Inspector Paul Jones in *Nurses Who Kill*, Episode 1, Director Chris Jury. Training: Rose Bruford College.

Christine Hancock, originally from Essex, lived in Rugby for over forty years. A passion for Family History led to an interest in local history, especially that of the town of Rugby. In 2013 she joined a class at the Percival Guildhouse with the aim of writing up her family history research. The class was Writing Fiction and soon she found herself deep in Anglo-Saxon England. Based on the early life of Byrhtnoth, Ealdorman of Essex, who died in 991AD at the Battle of Maldon, the novel grew into a series. She self-published four volumes followed by the first volume of a new series, *The Wulfstan Mysteries*.

Sadly Christine passed away in December 2021. We remember her with great fondness.

Kate A Harris and her three siblings lived on their farm near Market Harborough. She left home at 16 to pursue her career with children. After training in the Morley Manor, Dr. Barnardo's Home, in Derbyshire from 1966 to 1968, she qualified as a Nursery Nurse. Kate met and married her Royal Naval husband in Southsea when working in a children's home. As a naval wife, she was in Malta for two years with her two sons when they were shutting the naval base. They have two sons and two grandchildren. She worked on the local newspaper and discovered a love of writing at 50! Now she is writing her story mainly featuring Barnardo's. It's a major challenge with intense and fascinating research. She's had an incredible response from diverse and fascinating resources. Kate is interested in hearing from people who worked in Barnardo's, mainly in the 1960s.

Cathy Hemsley has been writing short stories and full-length novels for over twelve years: inspired by her family history and by her child's idea for a fantasy novel. Two of her stories have been published in *The People's Friend* and she has completed a fantasy duology, *The Gifts* and *The City*, as well as a book of short stories, *Parable Lives*, all available on Amazon. She is now retired from paid work, working on another two novels, supporting a local church, growing organic vegetables, and is also helping local people as the Rugby advocate for the Acts435 charity.

Jim Hicks was born and raised in Rugby. After leaving school, he studied computing at Imperial College, London and the University of Cambridge. He worked in the Computing Services department of the University of Warwick for nearly twenty-six years before being made redundant in 2011. His mother is a little surprised that he joined a writers' group. He thought someone might want some help with the technical side of using a computer to prepare documents, and has remained ever since.

John Howes was born and raised in Rugby. He was a journalist on local newspapers for 25 years before retraining as a teacher. He has self-published two books – *We Believe*, a collection of his writings on spirituality, and a guide on how to teach poetry. He plays the piano and writes music for schools and choirs. John is working on a memoir and dabbles in poetry. He runs a book group and a lively theology group. He presents a Youtube Channel dedicated to the music of Elton John.

Ruth Hughes was born in Sutton Coldfield but has lived in Rugby for 50 years. She says, "I think I have a book in me but so far I just enjoy writing poems and recollections of my life." Ruth belongs to Murder 57, which enacts murder mysteries around the country, and to Rugby Operatic Society.

Chloe Huntington started writing at the age of five or six and since then she hasn't stopped. She has written short stories for school projects and essays for homework, but she has never published any of her works. She hopes that she can one day publish one (or more) of her stories and introduce the world to her world of fantasy, fiction and romance. Chloe lives with her Mum and her six chickens and wants to hopefully write a story from the point of view of a dog that she loves. What will Chloe write next?

Rosemary Marks has lived in Rugby all her life and has three children and three grandchildren. She has always been an avid reader and was lucky enough to work at Rugby Library for 23 years, a Bibliophile's dream. She is now retired and enjoys travelling with her husband, writing, painting, researching her family history and spending time with friends and family.

Madalyn Morgan was brought up in a pub in Lutterworth, where she has returned after living in London for thirty-six years. She had a hairdressing salon in Rugby before going to Drama College. Madalyn was an actress for thirty years, performing on television, in the West End and in Repertory Theatre. She has been a radio journalist and is now presenting classic rock on radio. She has written articles for music magazines, women's magazines and newspapers. She now writes poems, short stories and novels. She has written ten novels – a wartime saga and a post war series. She is currently writing her memoir and a novel for Christmas 2023.

Fran Neatherway grew up in a small village in the middle of Sussex. She studied History at the University of York and put her degree to good use by working in IT. Reading is an obsession – she reads six or seven books a week. Her favourites are crime, fantasy and science fiction. Fran has been writing for thirty-odd years, short stories at first. She has attended several writing classes and has a certificate in Creative Writing from Warwick University. She has completed three children's novels, as yet unpublished, and is working on the first draft of an adult novel. Fran has red hair and lives in Rugby with her husband and no cats.

Simon Parker grew up and lived on The Wirral until 1985. He arrived in Rugby in 2003 via Coventry, Bristol and Seattle. He's an aerospace engineer by training, with a love of the open road whether by bicycle, motorcycle or car. His travels galvanise his writing and he writes fiction for pleasure. He lives with his wife, two teenage children and a small collection of interesting vehicles: 'on the button' and ready for their next adventure!

Steve Redshaw was born and raised in Sussex. Over the past forty years he has taught in primary schools in the South of England and East Anglia. Now retired, he is living aboard his narrowboat, Miss Amelia, on the Oxford Canal near Rugby. Passionate about music, he sings and plays guitar in pubs, folk clubs and sessions around the area. He also is a dance caller for Barn Dances and Ceilidhs. His creative output is perhaps best described as emergent and sporadic, but when inspiration strikes, he finds himself writing songs, poems and short stories.

Chris Rowe. Just before covid, Chris tried to write poetry: lockdown gave the time to attempt different poetic forms, some of which appeared in Press Pause. From childhood, Chris has been interested in reading prose: such as Richmal Crompton (Just William), Alison Utley (Sam Pig), Henry Fielding, Mark Twain, Jane Austen, and Terry Pratchett. Shakespeare has always been a favourite and long ago the ambition was achieved of seeing a performance of every play: Antony and Cleopatra being the hardest to track down (all those scene changes deter production.). Favourite performers of the Bard are Oddsocks.

Christopher Trezise was born and raised in Rugby and pursued a professional acting career on theatre stages culminating in work for Disneyland Paris. Christopher has held many jobs from kitchen assistant through to risk management consultant but he has always had a passion for writing. He runs several table-top roleplaying groups which he writes scenarios for and has self-published a fantasy book based upon one of those games.

Lindsay Woodward has had a lifelong passion for writing, starting off as a child when she used to write stories about the Fraggles of *Fraggle Rock*. Knowing there was nothing else she'd rather study, she did her degree in writing and has now turned her favourite hobby into a career. She writes from her home in Rugby, where she lives with her husband and cat. When she's not writing, Lindsay runs a Marketing Agency, where she spends most of her time copywriting, so words really are her life. Her debut novel, *Bird*, was published in April 2016, and Lindsay's 9th novel is due to be released in 2023.

Chris Wright says the following:
My earliest memory is of my mother using flashcards
to teach me to read while still in my playpen
we lived in a flat at West Heath,
a Vimto only area of Birmingham,
so my poetry is restricted
to about fifty different words
usually including "hippopotamus"